Styal, Cheshire

A SMALL village on the River Bollin near Wilmslow, mainly populated by people who work in nearby Manchester, during the industrial revolution to house mill workers, Styal is still a thriving community.

Quarry Bank in Styal is part of the National Trust and visitors to the cotton mill there, powered by Europe's most powerful working waterwheel, have the opportunity to step into the past. The sheer noise of the clattering and whirring of heritage machinery and steam engines is incredible. Make sure you book a tour with one of the knowledgeable guides and discover the fascinating story of how the cotton industry progressed from the mediaeval era through to the 19th century.

Wildlife abounds in the woodlands of Styal and rangers on the estate strive to maintain an environment that supports a rich diversity of life, from bats to bluebells and more. Ask about their different walks – Southern Woods, Kingfisher Walk and Giant's Castle Walk – as each one covers different ground and shows you a different side of the estate. ■

3

Dear Readers . . .

It is with great pleasure that I welcome you to "The People's Friend" Annual 2017. With 25 brand-new short stories written by some of your favourite "Friend" authors. Beautifully illustrated by our team of talented artists, this book is packed with super reading to keep you entertained the whole year through.

We have seasonal poems sure to delight and uplift you, 10 fabulous watercolour paintings from J. Campbell Kerr and some fascinating facts about that popular topic of conversation, the weather.

I do hope you enjoy this year's Annual as much as we've enjoyed creating it!

Angela

Angela Gilchrist, Editor

Contents

Complete Stories

Poetry

p.93

p.121

J. Campbell Kerr Paintings

Weather Lore

A Quiet Hogmanay

by Suzanne Ross Jones.

BRODIE picked up the cup I had just washed and began to dry it. "What are your plans for later, Mum?"

It was my soldier son's first evening home in a while, and I'd cooked all his favourite foods to celebrate. Brodie had made short work of the meal, which I was grateful for when he had such a big night ahead of him.

I smiled at the question.

"I don't have any plans."

He frowned.

"You're not doing anything for Hogmanay?"

"Nope," I confirmed.

The fact was, I was looking forward to an early bedtime with a good book. My son wouldn't understand the appeal of that, though, not at his age.

He reached for the matching saucer and nodded.

"Right, a night in front of the TV for two it is. I'll ring Nate in a minute and tell him I'll be giving the rugby club a miss."

I looked up from the sink, shocked he would even suggest such a thing. I placed my hands, soapy from the washing up, firmly on my hips.

"You are not staying in!"

Brodie was only home for a few days, and he hadn't seen any of his friends for ages. There was no way he should be babysitting me when he ought to be out enjoying himself with them.

He frowned at me and shrugged.

"I'm staying put. You can't be here on your own."

"Of course I can, Brodie! Since you joined the Army I've been home on my own a lot, you know – and as you can tell I've been perfectly fine."

He shook his head, stubborn.

"It's Hogmanay. You shouldn't be celebrating on your own. No-one should."

I sighed. Couldn't Brodie tell that celebrating was the last thing on my mind? This had not exactly been my best year, what with the divorce and everything, and I had no wish to bid it a fond farewell. The fact was, I was going to be glad to see the back of it!

I put the clean and dried plates away and smiled at my son. I decided to be honest with him about my plans.

"Tomorrow morning I will wake up and toast a brand-new start," I promised him. "But tonight I intend to be fast asleep before the bells. So you see, you might as well go out."

Brodie looked thoughtful for a moment.

"OK," he agreed reluctantly. "If you're sure, that is."

I hadn't been surprised he had tried to talk me out of my desire for a quiet Hogmanay. I had raised my wonderful son to make the most of every opportunity – to enjoy life and live every moment to the maximum. It was possible he thought I was a hypocrite for retreating to lick my wounds on the biggest party night of the year.

✳　✳　✳　✳

"Nate's here, Brodie!" I called up the stairs to where Brodie was busy getting ready for the Hogmanay party at our local rugby club.

"He won't be long," I told Nate, ushering him into the kitchen.

As we waited for my son to appear, Nate made himself comfortable at the kitchen table. I busied myself cutting a mountain of sandwiches into triangles. It seemed ages since teatime and I didn't want the boys doing too much celebrating on empty stomachs.

"How is your father doing these days?" I asked Nate as I brought the sandwiches over and set them down in the centre of the table. "I haven't seen him in years."

Nate's father, Jimmy, had raised his son by himself. He'd become a school-gate dad, and had been part of the group of parents I'd made friends with. But as our children had grown, and everyone had started to work longer hours, we'd all drifted apart.

Nate reached for one of the sandwiches and gave a grin of thanks.

"Dad's great, though I worry he spends too much time on his own."

"Really?"

That didn't sound like the Jimmy I'd known from all those years ago. He had always been very sociable. I felt a twinge of guilt that I hadn't made enough of an effort to keep in touch with everyone.

"He'll even be spending tonight on his own. Daft, I call it." Nate took another bite of his sandwich.

"There's a lot to be said for spending time in your own company," I told him. "You mustn't worry. He'll be fine."

Nate nodded.

"Brodie said you didn't have any plans for tonight, either."

I smiled.

"By the time you get to our age you'll probably appreciate an occasional quiet night in, too."

I sat down opposite him, hoping Brodie wouldn't be too much longer. Nate was a lovely boy, but I was keen to get back to my book.

Nate shook his head.

"It just seems a shame."

"What does?"

"You both spending New Year's Eve alone."

"Sometimes that's just how life works out." I got to my feet. "Why don't I make you a cup of tea to wash down that sandwich?"

"My dad had a soft spot for you, you know." Nate's voice came from behind me as I filled the kettle.

I smiled and turned to face him.

"I was very fond of your father, too."

"In fact, he . . ."

Nate stopped mid sentence as my son appeared in a cloud of aftershave. And I never did find out what it was he had been going to say.

A short while later, I was heading to bed when the doorbell rang. A glance at the clock showed me it was only ten-thirty, so far too early for first footers.

I opened the door cautiously.

"Jimmy!"

Even if I had been thinking of him after my chat with his son earlier, I was still very surprised to see Nate's dad after all these years.

"Hello, Rachel." He'd always had a nice smile and he used it to good effect now. "Have I missed the boys or are they still here?"

"I'm afraid they've gone." I pulled the door wider and stood aside. "But come in out of the cold."

"The thing is, Nate forgot his wallet." He held it aloft as he walked in. "He left it on the hall table. I was hoping I would catch him here. His mobile's switched off and, well, I didn't think that I could face the rugby club on New Year's Eve!"

I led the way into the kitchen and got out two glasses and a bottle of wine. Well, it was Hogmanay, after all.

"Don't worry, Jimmy. Brodie will see he's all right."

His face cleared.

"Of course he will. I should have thought about that."

"Well, I'm glad you didn't." I poured drinks for us both. "It's so nice to see you again. If you've got a few minutes, why don't we go into the living-room and we can catch up?"

JIMMY'S life since we had last chatted, it seemed, had been as uneventful as mine had been turbulent. But the end result had been the same, for here we both were, on our own on Hogmanay.

"Your ex must be mad, you know," he told me when we had polished off the wine. "I can't believe he would leave someone like you."

For a moment I didn't know what to say. Perhaps it was the wine talking. But then I recalled what Nate had said earlier. I hadn't given it much thought at the time, but as I looked into Jimmy's eyes now, I felt that, maybe, Nate had been trying to tell me something significant.

I felt my face grow warmer.

"I reckon it's all for the best," I told him with an attempt at levity. "After all, if he hadn't gone and left me we wouldn't be sitting here now."

It was crazy logic and we both laughed. It was good to be happy.

"Look at that," I said, pointing to the clock on the mantelpiece. "It's after midnight."

After everything, the old year had ended so painlessly that I hadn't even noticed. It might not have been the way I'd planned, but I'd started this year laughing – and that had to be good.

And while I wasn't sure it would ever lead to anything, it was good to know a nice man found me attractive.

"Happy New Year." I smiled across the sofa at him.

It seemed entirely natural for us both to lean a little closer for a traditional New Year kiss.

Somehow, without meaning to, it turned into something a bit more than a peck.

And suddenly the New Year and the new start I had been so looking forward to were looking even better. ∎

Clowning Around

by Vivien Hampshire.

T HE first time I set eyes on Mark Thomas he was dressed as a clown. Spotty trousers, big yellow shoes, curly blue wig, painted face, squeaky red nose – the lot! In fact, as I sat huddled on a bench overlooking the sea and turned to watch him handing out leaflets to passers-by and leaping about, squirting streams of water at laughing children from a fake flower on his lapel, I just assumed he was a real clown.

In a seaside town like ours it wasn't unusual for a circus to pitch up every now and then, and I thought they must have sent this clown on ahead to drum up some business.

It was a chilly winter's morning. I had been hoping to snatch a few minutes' peace and quiet and some fresh air during my break, but the wind was starting to blow up and I was thinking of heading back to work. People were hurrying away, dipping inside shops and cafés to get out of the wind, and as most of his potential customers gradually disappeared the clown shook his head, tucked the remainder of his leaflets into his belt and clopped his way across the deserted prom towards me.

"Mind if I sit down?" he asked, pulling his nose off and slipping it into his pocket. "My feet are killing me."

Well, when I looked down at those incredibly large shoes and thought just how heavy and uncomfortable they must be, I couldn't help but laugh out loud.

"Of course not," I said, pointing at the empty half of the bench beside me. "Plenty of room. Help yourself."

"I don't normally dress like this, you know," he said after a few moments of awkward silence, during which I had given up trying to read my magazine in the blustery wind and he had eased his feet out of the enormous shoes and was wiggling his toes up and down with relief.

"No, I didn't think you did. Not all the time, anyway!"

Then I burst into a fit of giggles, and his colourfully made-up face cracked into a smile. His blue eyes sparkled cheekily at me, and somehow the ice was broken.

Illustration by Ruth Blair.

"Would you like a biscuit?" I said, offering the open packet to him with a smile.

"Thanks. I never say no to food! And would you like one of these?" He pulled out a leaflet and passed it to me, trying to speak through a mouthful of garibaldi crumbs. "Special discounts all this week."

"Oh, I'm not sure. You don't use live animals, do you?"

"No, they've usually been dead for quite a while by the time I get my hands on them!"

"What? That's terrible! Whatever sort of circus do you work for?"

"Oh, no! You thought I was a real clown?"

He looked aghast.

"Sorry. No, perhaps I should explain. It's my new restaurant I'm promoting. Nothing to do with a circus at all. I'm Mark. Restaurant owner, chef and occasional clown."

"I'm Ting." I could feel myself redden at getting things so wrong. "Paediatric nurse, line dancer and occasional idiot!"

I held out my hand and he took it, raising it to his painted lips and kissing

11

it dramatically, which just made me giggle again even more than I had the first time.

"Easy mistake to make, I suppose, so you're certainly not an idiot. But a line-dancing nurse, eh? Sounds intriguing. As does your beautiful name."

"My mother is Chinese. She chose it because it means graceful, which I try to be when I dance. It's not always easy when I'm wearing my cowboy boots, though! It's just a hobby, the line dancing, but I enjoy it. So you're a chef?"

"Yes. That started out as a hobby, too, but it's serious now. I've put my life savings into this new place. We're opening tomorrow."

"I see. That sounds exciting. But how does the clown costume fit in, exactly?"

"Take a look at the name of the restaurant."

I peered at the piece of paper in my hand.

"Coco's?"

"I thought it sounded warm, friendly and fun, and that it might make people think about cosying up by the fireplace with a nice comforting mug of cocoa or hot chocolate. That's the sort of atmosphere I'm hoping to achieve.

"Then there's Coco the clown. Yes, I know the fancy dress is a bit over the top, but marketing's everything these days, isn't it? I'm new in town, so I'm not going to get customers through the door on the strength of my cooking alone. I felt I needed a gimmick – something they wouldn't forget in a hurry."

I nodded.

"You've certainly managed that."

"So, Ting, will you come? It's half price on all main courses this week, and free desserts if you use the voucher. I could do with the support, just in case nobody else turns up!"

"I'm sure they will," I said reassuringly.

He shrugged.

"Bring a friend, husband, boyfriend, whatever! I have some nice little tables for two. Candles, flowers, the works."

"Er, that won't be necessary. There's no-one special in my life right now. I'm actually working long shifts at the moment so I don't finish until late in the evening. All I want to do then is go home and put my feet up. But I could try to come later in the week."

"Of course. Let me know when and I'll make sure you're well looked after."

Then he slipped his feet back into the big yellow shoes and hobbled away, waving as he went. I spent the next few minutes, as I made my way back to the hospital, wondering just what my new clown friend might look like when the costume and the make-up were off. Judging by the twinkle in those piercing blue eyes, I had a feeling I was going to be pleasantly surprised.

* * * *

Coco's restaurant was lovely. From the soft creamy décor and crackling flames of the real log fire to the heavenly smells wafting across from the small kitchen area at the back, I loved it from the moment I walked in.

"Mark's expecting you," a young waitress said when I hovered at the reservations desk and gave her my name. "Follow me."

I hadn't been sure about coming in here by myself, but Mark had arranged for me to sit at a sweet little table in the corner, where I didn't stick out like a sore thumb but still had a perfect view of the rest of the room. I enjoyed watching the other diners coming and going, the waiters and waitresses popping over every now and then to top up my glass with complimentary champagne, and the soft music that played in the background, keeping my toes tapping away under the table.

The food was wonderful, too.

"My compliments to the chef," I said as a waitress whisked away my dessert bowl and spoon. I wondered just how many pounds I had put on around my waist since I'd arrived. "That was all absolutely delicious."

"Why, thank you, madam," a voice said from somewhere behind me as a man appeared, pulled over a chair and sat down opposite me. "I am so glad you enjoyed it, and I very much hope you will come again."

"Mark? Is that you?"

"What, you don't recognise me in my chef's whites?" He chuckled.

"Not without the wig and make-up, no! What a fantastic restaurant you have. I've really enjoyed being here. Well done."

He positively glowed with pleasure.

"Thanks. I'm pretty much done in the kitchen now. All the mains have been served, and my assistant can cope with the last few desserts. Luckily we have machines to do the washing-up! Please take this, as a swap for the garibaldi biscuit you gave me the other day." He slipped a small foil-wrapped chocolate mint, emblazoned with Coco's logo, in front of me. "And if you don't mind me sitting here we could share a pot of coffee before I quickly get changed and drive you home."

"There's no need to do that. The bus . . ."

"On a dark night like this? And you travelling alone? Absolutely not. I invited you, so I'm going to make sure you get home safely. You can put that purse away, too. Your meal is on the house tonight. No arguments."

I took a long look at his face. As I'd suspected, it was extremely good-looking, and those blue eyes of his shone expectantly at me as we sipped our drinks. There would be no argument from me, that was for sure.

"Fine. I give in. But on one condition."

"Name it."

"That next week you put your clown suit on again, and come along to help me out with something at the hospital."

THAT'S how we came to be here in the children's ward this afternoon: Mark in his clown outfit and me in my line-dancing boots with the tassels, and wearing my cowgirl hat. We're entertaining the children at the party I've organised every February since I first started working here. It's Chinese New Year, and even though I'm half English I still like to keep up the old Chinese traditions I learned from my mum.

Some of the children are confined to bed, some are in wheelchairs, some have to lug their drips or their oxygen around wherever they go, but that doesn't stop them having fun. I tell them a few Chinese folk stories from the books I've brought, and then we sit at a table with heaps of coloured card and scissors and sticks of glue, and make traditional Chinese paper lanterns.

Mark goes from bed to bed, squirting water from his flower and letting the kids squeeze his false nose until it squeaks. After that we start the dancing, lining them all up along the middle of the ward and draping a huge golden cloth over everyone, so we resemble a long pulsating dragon as we all dance together. Meanwhile the nurses start to dish up plates of noodles and pile up the fortune cookies for after we've finished.

"We've never had a clown at our parties before, Mark," I tell him when it's all over and we're sitting together in the staff room, the children all tired out and resting on their beds. "Thank you so much for coming."

"I've never danced with a cowgirl before, let alone a dragon! It's been fun. But I have to get changed and get the restaurant ready for evening service. Can I see you again later, do you think? Maybe for a drink after we close?"

"Will it be mugs of hot chocolate in front of the fire?"

"Why not?" He laughs. "Sounds good to me."

"Here. Open up the last fortune cookie. I saved it especially for you."

I watch him pull the cookie apart, read the slip of paper inside and smile, but he won't tell me what it says.

Then something quite magical happens.

My eyes are closed but I hear the staff-room door open, the sound of the charge nurse's shoes stopping abruptly, turning and retreating as she quietly closes it again and leaves us alone. After all, it's not every day you see a clown and a cowgirl kissing, each with a paper lantern hanging over one arm, and with a deflated golden dragon draped around their feet!

As I run my fingers through Mark's curly blue wig and accidentally make his big red nose squeak as I pull him closer, it no longer matters what the fortune cookie says. Suddenly my future looks very bright to me. ■

The North Wind Doth Blow

AS the days lengthen, so the cold strengthens," as the old saying goes, and it's often just as we see spring on the horizon that the weather in February turns bitterly cold. Part of the reason for this is that the wind in February often comes from the north-east, from the dry, cold continental winter air in Russia and Eastern Europe. Some folk call this a "lazy" wind, because it cuts through you rather than going round.

Contrary to popular belief, no matter how cold it gets it's never "too cold to snow." So long as there's moisture in the air, snow can fall in extremely cold temperatures. But cold weather is often associated with dry air, which is how this belief may have begun.

One way to tell whether winter is on its way out or not echoes the traditional rhyme:

"If Candlemas be fair and bright,
Winter will have another fight,
But if Candlemas Day be clouds and rain,
Winter is gone and will not come again."

Candlemas Day is February 2, which is also Groundhog Day in the USA, the day on which Punxsutawney Phil is brought out from his burrow on Gobbler's Knob in the town of Punxsutawney in Philadelphia. According to legend, if Punxsutawney Phil sees his shadow, there will be six more weeks of winter weather. If he does not see his shadow, there will be an early spring. The date is no coincidence – it came with Pennsylvania's earliest settlers observing their old custom of Candlemas Day. ●

To The One I Love

by Linda Lewis.

THE valentine was the kind Margaret's ex-husband used to send, with two entwined hearts and a cherub floating over them, bow in hand. She inspected the envelope, searching for clues, but didn't find any. There was no stamp, no postmark, nothing. Only words, carefully printed in capital letters. *TO THE ONE I LOVE.*

The card had obviously been delivered by hand. Carefully, she placed it on the mantelpiece and stepped back to admire it, all the time wondering who could have sent it.

The only person Margaret could think of was her neighbour, Howard. Once a month, they went to the book group together – it made sense to share the driving. She'd had no idea he had feelings for her; she'd never thought of Howard as a possible love interest. Standing five feet six in his socks, he was slightly shorter than she was, and apart from a love of reading they had little in common.

Since her divorce, she'd become resigned to life on her own. Besides, she'd always preferred men who were dark, and Howard was fair.

She sighed wistfully. At least somebody liked her enough to send a card.

Maybe it wasn't Howard. Maybe she'd caught the eye of a tall, dark, handsome stranger! Immediately the image of her boss jumped into her head. Mr Brown was the kind of man she could see herself falling for, but he was way out of her league.

She chuckled. As if, at fifty-two, she was even in a league!

As she got ready for work, Margaret found herself singing along to the radio. Instead of the grey or black she normally wore, she selected a maroon skirt and a soft pink blouse. Margaret worked in the office over a supermarket, dealing with correspondence, replying to e-mails and sometimes talking to irate or disappointed customers.

As she turned on her computer, she kept thinking about the unexpected valentine card. Just the thought of that chubby little cherub made her smile.

"You seem cheerful this morning."

Mr Brown's voice startled her.

"Sorry? Yes, I suppose I am."

"Have you done something with your hair?" he asked. "You look different."

"Not really. I washed it last night." As soon as she said the words she realised how daft they sounded.

Mr Brown stood by her desk for what felt like ages, then he nodded.

"Have a good day," he said, then he disappeared into his office.

Illustration by Jim Dewar/Thinkstockphotos.

Margaret wondered what had got into him. Normally he only ever talked about work.

The strangeness of today didn't end there. A few minutes later a customer called, complaining that they'd stopped selling his favourite brand of coffee. At first he'd been quite cross, but Margaret soon smoothed his ruffled feathers.

"Thanks. You've been very helpful," he said at last. "What's your name?"

"Mrs Jenkins," she replied. "Margaret Jenkins."

"Oh, I'm sorry," he said quickly. "I didn't realise you were married."

"Actually I'm divorced." The phone went quiet. "Are you still there?"

"Yes. Sorry, I was wondering, could I buy you a drink some time?"

"You know nothing about me!" She laughed.

"So?"

"I'm fifty-two; I've got three grown-up children and two grandchildren." She paused. "Do you still want that drink?"

"I'm thirty-four, so maybe not." The man laughed. "You sound so much younger on the phone. Have a good day."

"You, too," Margaret replied.

It was the second time somebody had said that to her.

A GLANCE at the clock reminded her it was time for a break. As she walked past Mr Brown's office she saw the door was open. She looked in.

"Shall I bring you a coffee?"

To her surprise, he stood up.

"I'll come with you," he said.

Margaret didn't know what to say.

As they headed up to the staff-room, he suddenly smiled.

"I've figured out what's different about you. It's that blouse; the colour really suits you."

"Thank you."

Curiouser and curiouser, she thought.

When they reached the staff-room, they were the only ones there.

"Sit down," Mr Brown said, "and I'll make you one for a change. How do you take it?"

"Let me," she said, but he insisted.

It felt strange, waiting to be served coffee by her boss. She was relieved when two cashiers came up for their break.

"Thank you, Mr Brown," she said as he put the mug on the table.

"It's time you called me John," he said as he sat next to her.

"I'm not sure I can do that. You're my boss."

He leaned across the table.

"I'd like to be more than that. I was wondering, would you have dinner with me some time?"

Margaret had no idea what to say. It was like some kind of a dream.

"Well, OK," she managed at last. "I suppose I could."

John Brown sat back in his chair and nodded.

"I've been wanting to ask you out for months, but you always looked so sad, I didn't dare." He sipped his drink. "Today, though, I don't know what it is, but you're different somehow. Are you free on Saturday?"

"Saturday?" she repeated.

"Yes. For dinner. There's no point trying to find anywhere tonight. It's Valentine's Day."

"Yes," she managed.

"Good. I'll pick you up at eight." He checked his watch. "I'd better go. I'm expecting a call."

When he'd gone, Margaret replayed the morning's events over and over in her mind. It was only eleven a.m. and she'd already been asked out twice!

Just then the image of the valentine card popped into her head. She needed to do something about Howard. It was the book group that evening and it was her turn to drive.

*　*　*　*

She phoned him as soon as her break was over.

"Hi, it's Margaret."

Howard interrupted her.

"That's funny. I was going to call you later. I can't make the book group tonight." He paused. "I have a date."

"A date?"

"Yes. It's Valentine's Day. I finally found the courage to ask Shirley out to dinner. You could have knocked me down with a feather when she said yes! You don't mind too much, do you?"

"No, not at all. We'll miss you both at the group, of course." She cleared her throat. "Sorry if I sound a bit confused, only somebody put a valentine through my letter-box this morning." She paused. "This sounds silly now, but I thought it was you."

"Whatever gave you that idea? I mean, you're a lovely woman, Margaret, and we're good friends, but . . ."

"Don't worry about it. Like I said, I was just being silly. Good luck with your date."

As she hung up she felt flummoxed. If Howard hadn't sent the card, who had? It must have been one of her friends or a member of the family, hoping to cheer her up. Well, it had certainly done the trick; she was having a perfectly wonderful day!

THAT evening, as she was making up her mind what to have for dinner, a knock came at the door. When she opened it, she found a young couple standing there.

"Excuse me," the man said. "This is going to sound weird, but did you get a valentine card this morning? Pink, with hearts and a cherub?"

"Yes, I did. Why?"

"I think it could be mine. I asked my kid brother to drop it off on his way to school. This is Manston Crescent and my girlfriend lives in Manston Close."

"Hang on," Margaret said. "I'll go and fetch it."

She went inside, took the card from the mantelpiece and showed it to the young man.

"See?" He turned to his girlfriend. "I told you I'd sent you one!"

Then he sank to his knees.

"Dora, darling, I love you so much. Will you marry me?"

The girl's reply was to throw her arms round his neck. Margaret guessed that meant yes. She held out the card.

"Here, take it. It's yours."

But the girl shook her head and gave her new fiancé a squeeze.

"When he guessed what had happened, he bought me another one."

A quick rummage in her handbag produced an identical card, which she showed to Margaret.

"I don't need two, so you can keep it, if you like."

"Thank you," Margaret replied as the couple turned to go.

She clutched the valentine to her heart. It was just a card; it hadn't even been meant for her. But somehow it had brought love back into her life. ▪

Spring Has Sprung

S IGNS of spring are often seen long before March, but it's the beginning of the month that interests weather buffs. "In like a lion, out like a lamb," the old saying goes – and the early days of March often do see stormy winds and gales. There's no guarantee of balmy weather by April, though!

The first day of spring isn't easy to pin down. Astronomers point to the vernal equinox, the time when the earth's path around the sun means that day and night are of equal lengths. This is around March 20 each year, give or take a little adjustment for leap years. Weather forecasters prefer four equal meteorological seasons of three months each, with spring beginning on March 1. In the past, farmers relied on natural signs to tell them how the seasons were progressing. So the onset of spring wouldn't be determined by the calendar but by signs such as the appearance of snowdrops, frogspawn, ladybirds and the first swallow to determine when the land locally would be in the right condition for ploughing and sowing.

Even so, it's possible for winter to make a late appearance. Met Office statistics show that snow is actually more likely at Easter than at Christmas! In the UK, snow or sleet falls on an average of five days in December, compared to six days in March. So, depending when Easter falls in a given year, we could be making snow bunnies as part of our celebrations! ●

Illustration by Ruth Blair.

A Random Act Of Kindness

by Keith Havers.

MARY wasn't in a particularly charitable humour as she trudged home from her job at the bakery. While most of the country was in festive mood, still buoyed by the Queen's Coronation that summer, she just couldn't rise to the spirit of the season. Then she saw Billy.

The lad was about six that first time Mary spoke to him.

"Hello, your name's Billy, isn't it?"

He sat shivering on his own doorstep, legs blue with cold in his tattered black shorts. His moth-eaten jersey was no match for the chill December wind.

He nodded.

"Mum not back from work yet?"

A shake of the head.

"Maybe she's working overtime," Mary suggested. "Earning some extra money for Christmas."

Mary wasn't sure if Billy was aware of exactly where his mum was, but he would know she wasn't at the factory. Everyone in the street knew about Billy's mum and her struggle to make ends meet.

On market days, the Old Bull was licensed to stay open in the afternoon for the stallholders and she was often seen in the late afternoon trawling around the square looking for cheap cuts of meat when the vendors were keen to be away for a pie and a pint. Or maybe she would pick up a few scraggy-looking vegetables that no-one else wanted.

Billy had never known his dad, a seaman who had failed to return from his perilous occupation in the North Atlantic. Life was hard for mother and boy.

"Why don't you come along to my house and sit by the fire? It's only a few doors up. We can keep an eye out for your mum."

He seemed reluctant at first, but when Mary took his ice-cold hand in hers he scrambled to his feet and walked with her along the pavement.

"I'll get a nice big fire going and we can sit and have some toast, eh?"

Mary's fireside armchair seemed to swallow the lad up as he settled himself on to the soft velvet cushion. The colour began to return to his cheeks as he tucked into two thick buttered slices and a glass of warm milk.

Mary knew it must be hard bringing him up on her own, but it didn't seem fair of his mother to leave the lad out on his own for so long. Mary didn't like to judge, but she felt sorry for the boy. He didn't deserve this.

"I've got some cake in the larder. Have you got room for a slice?"

This time Mary was rewarded with a smile as well as vigorous nodding.

After Billy had gone Mary wondered if she should go and speak to his mum. Why couldn't she give him a spare door key or at least a decent overcoat? But Mary knew money was tight and guessed that she would only antagonise the woman if she was seen to be interfering. She decided to keep her own counsel.

Little did Mary realise what that first encounter with Billy would lead to. It set a precedent for the next few weeks, with Mary finding the boy at his front door every market day and inviting him along to sit by the fire. After being a good Samaritan once, she could hardly walk by the next time, could she?

ONCE Christmas was over and the dark days of January descended, Mary couldn't hold back any longer. One afternoon she sent Billy home in a camel duffel coat, bought for a few shillings at a jumble sale, and a pair of navy woollen gloves.

She waited several days for his mum to react. People didn't like to be thought of as charity cases in those parts. But none came.

She must be past caring, Mary decided. She supposed pride went out of the window when you were desperate.

Things carried on in this vein right through until Easter. Then one afternoon towards the end of April something surprising happened. Mary was listening to the latest Perry Como release on the wireless when she heard a tap on the door.

Billy stood there with a couple of bits of paper in his hand.

"What's up, Billy? This isn't your usual day. Is your mum all right?"

"She's asleep."

"You'd better come in."

Once settled in his favourite chair with a glass of orange squash on the side table, he explained the reason for his visit.

"I brought you these."

He held out a daffodil fashioned from a drinking straw and some green and yellow crêpe paper. In his other hand he offered a crayoned sheet.

"This is lovely," Mary told him. "Did you make it yourself?"

"At school." He nodded.

"And who is this in the picture?"

"That's Mum asleep in the chair, and that's you and me having milk and toast."

You didn't have to be a psychologist to work out where that image came from. Billy obviously regarded Mary as some sort of escape from a lonely home life.

She didn't know whether to feel proud or guilty.

"Shouldn't you give these to your mum?"

"I don't think she's interested."

He asked her to help him label the people in the picture. Mary found a soft-leaded pencil and helped him form the letters: *Billy, Mary and Mummy.*

From that point on, Billy's visits didn't just occur on market days. His mum didn't seem to mind that he often spent a good part of the evening or Sunday afternoon at Mary's house. In addition, Mary's hospitality had extended to giving him a cooked meal and keeping him entertained.

"Do you like drawing?" she asked one afternoon.

"Sometimes," he replied. "But I like making things, too."

A sketch pad, coloured pencils and some Plasticine gave Billy hours of enjoyment as he sat in Mary's living-room. Mary, too, gained a lot of pleasure from his company. She soon recognised that the young chap had some artistic talent, but she worried for his future.

She was right to be concerned. Events soon conspired to bring an end to this idyllic period of her life.

One evening Mary was sitting in her living-room wondering why Billy hadn't called round to listen to "Children's Hour". She was about to switch from the "Light Programme" to the "Home Service" when there was a knock at her door.

"Have you heard what's happened?" her neighbour on the doorstep asked. "There's been an accident at the factory. Billy's mum has been killed."

It took her a few seconds to respond.

"No! Are you sure? Where did you hear this?"

"I was in the snug at the Old Bull when someone shouted the news across the bar."

"What about Billy?"

"They say someone took him out of school this afternoon. I expect he'll have to go into foster care until they find him somewhere permanent. Poor little mite."

After a sleepless night Mary took time off work to try to find out where they had taken Billy, but the authorities weren't co-operative and she had to resign herself to the fact that he was gone. Several days later she discovered that relatives had been located and he had been sent to live with them.

FOUR years went by and Mary had pushed all memories of Billy to the back of her mind. Only at Christmas and Easter would she be reminded. Then, out of the blue, a letter dropped on her doormat. The script was neat and obviously written using a fountain pen. Billy was proud to announce that he had passed his eleven-plus and would be going to grammar school in the autumn. His aunt and uncle were finding it hard to kit him out with all the necessary equipment, but they were managing.

What a relief, Mary thought. It sounded like he had a decent home life at last.

Billy hadn't put his address on the letter and the envelope had a Birmingham postmark, so Mary wasn't much wiser as to where he was living.

Mary looked forward to receiving more news, but all she received over the next six years were Christmas cards. At least he was keeping in contact.

Then she received another letter. Billy was about to take his O-levels and his teachers predicted top grades for him. His favourite subject was still art, but he was also studying several languages. He included his address this time and Mary had no hesitation in sending a reply. By this time she had had a telephone installed and she included her number in the hope that he would call.

Two weeks later she answered the phone and heard the sound of coins being fed into a public phone box.

"Is that Mary?"

His voice was deeper but she knew it was him.

"Billy! How are you?"

As they chatted Mary noticed that his accent had changed, too.

"I'm sorry I didn't write more," he said. "My uncle and auntie had to move around a lot."

Mary had read about the big clear-out of the Birmingham suburbs. Old housing had been demolished and whole communities scattered to outlying towns.

A Note To My Optician

I'D like some special specs, please,
To help me see with ease
Just where I left my notebook,
Just where I left my keys.
They need not see the bad things,
Like when my clothes look tight,
But just the smiles and sunshine
That help my world look bright.
And could you find some frames, please,
To make me look – "Oh, wow!"?
A bit more like a film star,
And less a startled cow.
It can't be much to ask, please,
To sort out these affairs.
Just ring me when they're done, please.
I want a hundred pairs!

– Maggie Ingall.

"How's school?"

"I had to move school, but I'm settled into one now."

From then on Billy rang every couple of weeks.

"I passed all my exams!" he reported one night before even saying hello.

"Congratulations! I knew you would do well."

A few weeks later she had to console him when a girl he liked started dating another boy.

"You're young," she told him. "You'll probably have several girlfriends before you find the right one for you."

One night he told her he had gained a place at art college.

"Well done," she said, though she worried he would be moving yet again.

Mary longed to see him. The occasional photograph had given her an idea of how he was changing, but the black and white images were no substitute for the real thing.

He'll have changed in other ways, she thought. I do hope he's as kind and thoughtful as when I knew him.

Mary didn't have to wait long to find out.

"I'm exhibiting my work up here in Manchester," he told her in a call one night. "And I'd like you to be my special guest."

"I'd love to," Mary replied with no hesitation.

A LMOST thirty now, Billy had been teaching art at a Manchester college for several years, but now his own artistic efforts had been recognised.

Mary made the long journey up by train, but was slightly disconcerted when she arrived at the venue. Having expected the event to take place in an established gallery, she found herself following a small crowd down a side street and into what appeared to be a disused warehouse. Shabby light fittings hung from bare rafters and flakes of paint hung off the walls.

She stood amongst the exhibits feeling a little bewildered.

"I'm so glad you made it," Billy told her as soon as he spotted her.

Mary was treated as an honoured guest as he showed her around. After introducing her to his sponsor and a few of the other guests, he drew her to a quiet corner so that they could have a proper talk.

"Your work is very impressive," Mary told him. "I'm so proud of you."

"You set me on the road to this," he replied. "Do you remember that first time you found me on the doorstep?"

"You looked so alone and vulnerable."

"I was lonely. But my mum loved me in her own way. She just didn't have the energy or the opportunity to spend much time with me."

"That still must have been hard for a young boy to comprehend," Mary said.

"She couldn't help the situation she was in," Billy continued. "She did her best, but it was too much for her."

"You're a very kind son," Mary returned. "Not everyone would be so understanding."

"And not everybody would take in someone else's child and give them a hot meal."

They stood in silence for a few moments, reflecting on a time long gone. Billy noticed Mary's eyes wandering around the room.

"It's not what you were expecting, is it?"

"Well, I –"

"It's OK." He laughed. "It's not exactly the Tate Gallery, I know. But I have plans for this place."

"Here?" Mary asked. "I assumed you'd hired this building just for tonight."

"Not at all," Billy explained. "I've been awarded a local grant to spruce it up and open it as a youth club."

"You mean you're giving up teaching?"

"Far from it," he replied. "This is an extra-curricular project."

"I see."

"Even now kids are left to fend for themselves," he went on. "My mum had to work to put food on the table and a roof over our heads, and some still do. I want to provide a place for kids to go. They can come here to paint or build models. I'm hoping to provide table tennis and chess. Or they can just get a cup of tea and sit and chat."

"It sounds like a marvellous idea!"

"It's all because of what you did for me. You offered me a place to go when I needed it most."

Mary blushed as he went on.

"And do you know what I'm going to call it?"

Mary shook her head.

"I'm calling it the Doorstep, because that's where you found me, shivering in the cold and damp."

"I don't know what to say," Mary whispered with a tear in her eye. "I feel even prouder of you now."

Then she remembered something. She opened her bag and took out a limp paper daffodil and a faded crayon drawing.

"You kept them?" Billy asked.

"Apart from my memories and the letters, they're my only link with you."

"You're wrong," he said. "The link that ties us together is the fact I'm here. I can't imagine what would have happened to me if it weren't for my Good Samaritan."

MARY cast her mind back to that freezing afternoon, just before Christmas, 1953. She remembered wanting to get home as quickly as she could after an early morning start at the bakery and almost walking straight past the young lad huddled against the door frame.

Even now she couldn't recall what had made her pause and speak to him. She didn't feel like a Good Samaritan, just someone who couldn't walk away, no matter how reluctant she was to get involved.

Yet because of that small act of kindness there would be many more young boys and girls who didn't have to hang around on the street.

"They say no act of kindness is ever wasted," Billy said. "I can't pay you back for what you did for me. All I can do is pass it on."

Tears welled in Mary's eyes. She realised the kindness wasn't just being passed on. It was spreading out like ripples on a pond, and that was repayment enough. ■

Eriskay, Scotland

THIS small island in the Outer Hebrides has a very well-known claim to fame. It was, after all, off the shores of Eriskay that the *SS Politician* foundered in 1941, and the local seafaring community set sail to rescue her cargo of whisky. Compton Mackenzie told the tale in his book "Whisky Galore", and a film of the same name was made in 1949.

Who could resist the tale of thousands of bottles of whisky being hidden from the authorities by the wily islanders? Make sure you pay a visit to the Am Politician Lounge in Balla while you're on the island, as there is an original bottle of the whisky brought ashore from the ship displayed behind the bar.

That's not its only claim to fame, though. A small island of only three square miles off the coast of South Uist in the Outer Hebrides, Eriskay was also the first place where Prince Charles Edward Stuart – Bonnie Prince Charlie – set foot on Scottish soil back in 1745. ■

Illustration by David Young.

The Inside Story

by Pat Posner.

I'M not used to being head organiser of big events, Gloria." Edith Turner glanced around their living-room at the prefab villagers who'd come to discuss the Easter Fun Day being held in Broome Hall's grounds.

"One reason they chose you, Mum, is that they thought you'd find it easy to discuss arrangements with her. You know her better than any of them, what with Dad being her chauffeur."

"And everything has gone well so far, Edith, love," Bill said.

This was the last meeting until the day. Edith hoped it would go smoothly.

"Right, everyone. The countdown starts tomorrow when we'll make papier-mâché eggs and plaster of Paris Easter bunnies in Broome Hall's big barn. They'll dry overnight, to be decorated ready for Thursday's competition. Which," she added, "as you all know, is Fun Day. The judging will take place first thing. Her ladyship has got a TV actor coming to judge and award prizes."

"After that," Gloria added, "we'll sell our decorated eggs and bunnies along with other Easter goodies. There will be musical performances as well. It's been advertised in the local newspapers for the last three weeks now so hopefully there will be a large crowd."

"You'll be glad to know our hens are laying well," Mary Clayton said. "I'll have plenty of fresh eggs to sell."

"And I've made some wooden chicks," Sam Noble called.

"That's grand," Bill said. "One way or another, someone from every prefab in the village is playing a part."

It was almost midday before they finished making sure they all knew who was doing what. Still, hopefully a good amount of money would be raised towards the building of Broome Park's children's holiday home.

"I've just time for another cup of tea, love," Bill said. "Then I'm off to the station to fetch that reporter who'll be stopping at the hall. Her ladyship was chuffed when he phoned to ask if he could get the inside story. He'll take photos from start to finish. No doubt there will be a photograph of her ladyship wearing her egg jewellery in his posh magazine," he added, smiling at Gloria.

"There's already been photographs of it in magazines," Gloria told him. "I've cut them out to take to the barn on Wednesday – they'll give us ideas for decorating our papier-mâché eggs."

"We've two dozen moulds for making the Easter bunnies," Edith said. "I hope the youngsters understand that everything made will be on sale on the stalls!"

"Stop worrying, Edith," Bill said. "Her ladyship has an Easter bunny outfit. The person wearing it will hand out a chocolate egg to every youngster. Everything will be fine, you'll see."

NEXT morning, Gloria was making her way down Blakeley Road when Janet Whittaker hurried towards her.

"I'm going up to Broome Hall to help with the sandwiches for everyone making the eggs and rabbits in the barn. Are you going there, Gloria?"

"I was there earlier, checking everything was laid out ready. Then I had an errand to run. I'm on my way back now.

"Are you on the sandwich-making rota, too?"

"No. I'll be in the big barn, making an egg. I saw a photograph of her ladyship's egg pendant in a magazine. I want to make a tiny egg and decorate it like that. But I had to go and buy herring roes for Tai-Lu."

"Tai-Lu?"

"Yes. One of her ladyship's guests named her Siamese after that cat on TV. Her ladyship had ordered cod roes specially, but that fussy cat won't eat them."

"Then I'm glad I saw you," Janet said. "I'd be nervous arriving on my own."

"Who's judging the egg contest?"

"Some actor who was in 'The Grove Family'."

"So far there's only the reporter from the magazine and two or three of her ladyship's friends at the hall. And Tai-Lu's owner. The actor's coming tomorrow afternoon, but everyone else will arrive early on Fun Day."

They chatted on until they reached the hall.

"I'll bring these in for Tai-Lu and then get on with making my egg."

"Shall we walk home together as well, Gloria?"

"We could, though I said I'd wait and tidy the barn when we're done."

It was five o'clock before everyone went home. Gloria heaved a sigh of relief. Now she'd be able to set to and clear up. Half an hour later she'd just finished wiping the old wooden work benches when Janet came in with Tai-Lu on a harness.

"Her ladyship asked me to take her for a walk while her guests get changed for dinner. I had to fetch Tai-Lu from her owner's room, though I felt a right twerp when I went along the wrong corridor."

"It's such a rambling old place, it's easy to lose your way," Gloria agreed.

"That reporter did this morning. I took a cup of tea up for one of the guests and saw him outside her ladyship's rooms. He almost dropped his camera when he noticed me there. Said he was looking for his room to fetch a new roll of film."

"He took loads of photos. Made a bunny as well." Gloria laughed. "He got in a right mess. Any road, Janet, we'll never get home if I don't get this floor swept."

"If you've another broom, I'll help," Janet offered.

Tai-Lu jumped elegantly on to the larger table. A few minutes later there was a crash followed by a yowl from Tai-Lu as she knocked one of the jars off the table.

"Jeepers! The rubber mould has come out of it!" Gloria pointed to the name tag. "It's the reporter's bunny. Jeremy. Because the moulds are all alike we put our names on them so that we'll paint the right ones tomorrow. I think the plaster of Paris has cracked," she added, feeling the outside of the mould.

"You could empty it out and make another one," Janet suggested.

"There's no plaster of Paris left. But I think there's a packet at home. I can take this mould with me, refill it and bring it back in the morning. In case I can't find any plaster of Paris at home I'll take my name off mine and stick Jeremy's on." Gloria found the rubber mould with her own name stuck on it. "He'll know no difference when he comes to paint it."

After locking the barn doors, Gloria put the key in her pocket and the pair left.

When she got home Bernard volunteered to mix the plaster of Paris.

"I need to empty the mould first," Gloria told him.

Bernard spread newspaper on the worktop and Gloria pressed the top of the rubber mould. Just the bottom half of the rabbit shape dropped out.

"I thought so," Gloria said. "It's broken in half, or maybe into three."

"It's a good job you realised the plaster had cracked," Bernard said. "That reporter would have hit the roof if it had come out broken in front of everyone."

"He's OK, really, Bernard."

"Huh! You didn't hear him telling me off for disturbing him. And I was only –"

"Hang on, what's this?" Gloria interrupted him.

A small Cellophane package had dropped out.

"It's her ladyship's egg pendant!" She gasped. "Jeremy must have stolen it!"

"Don't touch it, there might be fingerprints on it. It was clever, hiding it in the plaster of Paris. When her ladyship discovered it was missing the police would search everybody's room and find nothing. They'd never think of looking –"

"Bernard, fetch Policeman Ken from his prefab. Then go and get Janet. She saw something earlier that the police need to know about."

"She isn't the only one," Bernard said as he hurried out.

✶ ✶ ✶ ✶

"So, Gloria," PC Boyce said a while later. "Let's go through it one more time. Are you positive this is the reporter's plaster rabbit?"

Gloria explained again how they'd all put their names on the moulds.

"Right. Janet, are you sure you saw the reporter outside her ladyship's rooms?"

"Yes. He looked embarrassed. I thought it was just because he had got lost."

"I bet it was because he'd been into the rooms and taken the pendant," Bernard said. "He yelled at me for disturbing him in the tack room. He said he was taking photos of old saddles, but I saw a rubber mould on the bench. I bet he'd filled it with wet plaster already and had gone to the tack room to hide the pendant in it."

"It doesn't make sense," Janet said. "How did he plan to get the rabbit away with him? They're all going on a stall to be sold afterwards. And he couldn't leave sooner since he's meant to be reporting the whole thing."

"He'd have bought his own rabbit," Gloria suggested.

When Bill Turner was told what was going on he decided to quietly ask her ladyship to check if her pendant was missing. It was a while before he returned.

"Well?" Gloria demanded, the second he walked in.

"Seems this here pendant was replaced by a fake. Her ladyship said it wasn't until she examined it really closely that she realised it wasn't hers."

"I bet someone copied it from a photograph," Gloria said.

"There's another thing, Ken," Bill said. "Her ladyship never asked which magazine he was from. Happen he isn't really a reporter at all!"

"Just a crook who saw the advertisement for the Fun Day in one of the newspapers and saw an opportunity," Gloria surmised.

"But we need to prove he's a crook," Bernard urged. "You're good at solving crimes, our Gloria. Can you think of some way we can catch him red-handed?"

"How long is he meant to be staying, Bill?" Policeman Ken asked.

"I was to take him to catch the six o'clock train on Thursday."

"It's lucky the barn's locked and I've got the key. If Jeremy's thinking of doing a runner tonight he'd have to break in, and he won't want to do that in case he gets caught. And, yes, I do have an idea." Gloria grinned.

She yawned as she unlocked the barn doors early the next morning. Everything was as she and Policeman Ken had left it last night. They'd placed the egg pendant into the rubber mould and filled it with plaster. She'd even remembered to stick Jeremy's name tag back on it. A policeman had hidden in the shadows all night in case Jeremy decided to break in and make a run for it.

Gloria put out what would be needed for everyone to paint their eggs or Easter bunnies. Now, she'd have to wait, and hope the next part of the plan worked well.

BEFORE long, the prefab villagers arrived, followed shortly after by Jeremy. He began to release his plaster bunny from its mould. Would the plaster be set for the bunny to be in one piece? Had they buried the Cellophane package deep enough?

Gloria needn't have worried. The bunny turned out perfectly.

An hour or so later, when they were busy painting, Gloria pointed.

"Look! It's the Easter Bunny!"

"I've come to give you all a chocolate egg for Easter," a deep voice said.

It had been Gloria's idea for Ken to wear the costume and give out the chocolate eggs. It would make it easy for him to keep an eye on Jeremy.

"There's a picnic in her ladyship's walled garden when we're finished," Gloria said to the little ones. "Shall we ask the Easter Bunny to join us?"

They all agreed. Bernard, who was staying close to Jeremy, grinned up at him.

"That'll make a great photograph for your magazine – all of us at the picnic with a big Easter Bunny. And the actor off the TV should be here by then as well."

Jeremy had no way of scarpering even if he'd been planning to, because once everyone had gone Gloria locked the barn doors. Tomorrow would be harder. They must be extra alert to make sure Jeremy didn't disappear after the judging.

Time passed quickly the following day. As Gloria guessed, after the judging Jeremy asked to buy the bunny he'd made. She said he could collect it at home time. Meanwhile they put it on the stall with a *Sold* sticker on it to encourage other folk to buy.

When people started leaving, Jeremy came to fetch his bunny. Bill appeared and told Jeremy he was ready to drive him to the station.

Later, in the Turners' kitchen, Gloria's dad smiled at her, Bernard and Janet.

"It went like clockwork. Jeremy didn't bat an eyelid when I said I was giving the Easter Bunny a lift, too. When Ken revealed his identity and demanded to see the plaster rabbit Jeremy confessed. He works for a gang who specialise in replacing genuine paintings and jewels with copies. They have a fake made and then either break in and swap the real thing for the fake, or a gang member gets a job in the place and waits for a chance to do the dirty work. They knew about the egg pendant, so when they saw the adverts for the Fun Day they came up with the plan of Jeremy pretending to be a reporter."

"But we rumbled him!" Bernard beamed. "Is he under lock and key now, Dad?"

"He is. And I'm off up to the hall to report to her ladyship and your mum."

"Tell Tai-Lu's owner I'll be up there in the morning with a huge pile of herring roes," Gloria said. "If Tai-Lu hadn't knocked over Jeremy's bunny mould . . ."

"We'd never have known the inside story," Bernard finished. ∎

What Mothers Do Best

by Emma Canning.

A HUGE smile spread over Maggie's face as she sauntered down the stairs and noticed a large white envelope lying on the doormat. It said *Mum* in Nathan's untidy scrawl. He must have taken a detour on his way to work to drop in a card for her. She bent to pick up the envelope. She wouldn't be seeing Nathan today, for he was a parent himself now, and understandably wanted to spend the evening with his own family.

Maggie tore open the envelope and pulled out the card. It pictured a china teapot, a plate of biscuits and a vase of delicate apricot-coloured roses. The verse inside it read:

There's one competition, Mum,
That you could never lose.
If I had to pick Best Mother
You're the one I'd always choose.
So relax and put your feet up,
It's a long time overdue.
Have a lovely day, and thank you, Mum,
For always being you!

Maggie grinned. Put her feet up? That was exactly what she planned to do.

Hurrying through to the kitchen to boil the kettle for tea, Maggie thought fondly of her children. Both were happy and settled. Nathan was married to Amy and they had a little daughter, Poppy, and Liv was away at university, working hard.

Maggie missed Liv dreadfully, but kept herself busy with a full-time job as manager of the local convenience store.

As Maggie poured hot water into the teapot, her husband Tom joined her in the kitchen.

"Morning, love," he said. "Had a nice lie-in?"

"Lovely. Look at the card Nathan dropped in."

Tom opened it and smiled.

"*Put your feet up*, it says. Is that what you're planning to do today?"

Illustration by Mandy Dixon/Thinkstockphotos.

Maggie nodded vigorously.

"Definitely. I'm going to enjoy a soak in the bath, then sit down with that novel I bought last week."

"Good idea. We're picking your mother up at five, aren't we?"

"That's right. The restaurant booking isn't till seven, but I thought we'd stop at Mum's for a while first. What are your plans?"

Tom grinned.

"I'm tidying the shed and the garage, so you'll have the house to yourself."

Maggie beamed. What a glorious thought!

✳   ✳   ✳   ✳

Amy smiled wearily as she gazed down at the folded piece of cardboard that Nathan had given her.

Her very first Mother's Day card! It was decorated with a dozen tiny footprints daubed in multicoloured paint. Nathan had even got Poppy to sign it with a messy orange handprint. Inside he had written, *Daddy will be cooking dinner tonight, so Mummy can put her feet up.*

Put her feet up? Oh, if only! Amy loved being a mother, but this week she was more tired than she'd ever been before. A cold was making Poppy restless and bad-tempered and, even though it was Sunday, Nathan had had to work. His long shifts at the hospital meant that they shared very few family weekends.

It was kind of Nathan to plan dinner later, but would there even be any food in the fridge for him to cook?

Amy kissed Poppy's hot forehead. The baby's cheeks looked far too red.

"Poor darling," Amy soothed, jiggling the unhappy baby on her shoulder. She wondered if she ought to call the doctor.

Perhaps she should phone Maggie. Amy had lost her own mother some years ago, but she was close to Nathan's mother. She reached for the phone, then paused, reluctant to interrupt the relaxing morning that she knew Maggie had planned.

Poppy's whimpers grew louder and Amy moaned in despair. Poppy was nearly seven months old and Amy felt she had coped well so far. She'd given up her job as a teaching assistant to be a full-time mum, and she'd thought she was doing a good job of being a mother.

But now – on Mother's Day of all days – it was all falling apart. Poppy's grizzles rose to a wail. Blinking back tears of her own, Amy stepped over the jumble of toys and pulled a baby book from her shelves.

Dorothy was sitting at her kitchen table reading the Sunday paper when the telephone rang.

"Hi, Mum, it's Maggie. Happy Mother's Day!"

"Thank you, dear. I'm looking forward to this evening. I've heard it's a splendid place. It sounds as though we were fortunate to get a booking."

"We were. Luckily, Tom knows the manager there, and he's saved us a table. We'll be with you at five o'clock. I thought we'd have a cup of coffee with you before we go. I'm having a nice relaxing day, and I hope you're doing the same. Make sure you put your feet up!"

"Oh, I will, don't you worry! See you later."

Dorothy put the phone down and sighed. Five o'clock seemed like an awfully long way off. What was she going to do until then? Despite what she'd told her daughter, she didn't want to put her feet up – she'd been doing far too much of that lately.

It was eight years since Dorothy's husband had died. Until recently she'd been content with her neighbours and friends for company, and family visits once or twice a week. But Sundays weren't the same since her granddaughter had gone away to university.

Liv used to call in every Sunday afternoon for tea and biscuits. It had become a habit since, aged fourteen, Liv had joined a choir that met every Sunday. She'd catch the bus into town and then, on her way home, would get off a few stops early and visit Dorothy. They'd play word games and do crosswords. Often the rest of the family would come over and join them for Sunday tea.

Looking back, Dorothy realised it had been the highlight of her week.

∗   ∗   ∗   ∗

Maggie, still pink from her hot, scented bath, was settling down with her book when Tom popped his head round the door.

"I think one of the car tyres has a puncture, love. I'll take it to the garage in town."

"I'll come, if you like," Maggie offered.

"No. You're meant to be putting your feet up."

Maggie beamed, kissed Tom and waved him off. She settled her slippered feet on the padded footstool and picked up her novel. Bliss!

Minutes later, the phone rang. The voice at the other end sounded tearful.

"Maggie, it's Amy. I'm so sorry to disturb you, but Poppy's not well. She's so hot and she won't stop crying. I don't know what to do!"

"Oh, Amy." Maggie considered. "Tom's taken the car or I would come straight over. Do you think Poppy needs a doctor?"

"I don't know!" Amy sobbed. "I'm pretty sure it's just a cold, but she's hardly slept for days."

"Neither have you, I suspect. How are you coping?"

"Not well," Amy admitted. She took a deep breath. "I do feel better for talking to someone. I'm just so tired."

Maggie listened sympathetically while Amy recounted the difficulties of her last few days.

"Would you like me to get a bus over to you, love?" she asked.

"No, it's all right, honestly. Thanks, Maggie. I feel better now and Poppy's settling down a bit, too."

Maggie smiled, hearing that Amy sounded calmer.

"Well, mothers usually know best," she said. "Perhaps she will sleep for a while."

"I think she might. Oh, Maggie, you should see the Mother's Day card Nathan and Poppy made for me. It's the cutest thing ever!"

"I'll see it when I pop in after work tomorrow," Maggie said. "Go and put your feet up. Get some rest while Poppy has a nap."

∗   ∗   ∗   ∗

Dorothy gave a cry of delight as she opened the door and found Liv standing on her doorstep, carrying a bunch of flowers and a gift bag festooned with purple ribbons.

"Hello, Gran! I'm making a surprise visit to Mum, so I thought I'd drop in on my way. I miss our Sunday biscuits."

"Come in, darling. Oh, I am glad to see you." Dorothy gazed with pleasure at the beautiful bouquet of lilac freesias, white roses and rich green foliage.

"The gift bag's for Mum. I'll put it here by the door. Don't let me forget it when I leave!"

"Your mum and dad are coming over," Dorothy told her, taking a tall glass vase from the cupboard under the sink.

"Well, I might as well stay and see them here."

"We're all going out to dinner. The restaurant will be busy, it being Mother's Day, but your dad knows the manager. I expect he'll be able to squeeze you in. Anyway, come and talk to me in the kitchen while I get busy making those biscuits!"

They chatted all afternoon. Dorothy listened as her granddaughter told her about her course and about life at university. What a lovely young woman she had become, Dorothy thought proudly. Only eighteen, but already so thoughtful and sensible.

Maggie and Tom arrived sharp at five o'clock, Tom in a smart suit and Maggie radiant in a flattering red dress. They were thrilled to find Liv at Dorothy's house, and there were hugs and kisses all round.

"This is grand," Tom said. "I'll phone the restaurant and see if they can fit you in."

"Thanks, Dad." Liv clasped her hands excitedly. "It'll be a treat."

"There's plenty of time for a cup of coffee before we go," Dorothy said. "Go and sit down and I'll fetch some."

Maggie led the way through to the sitting-room. It was spotless as usual: shining oak furniture and cream-coloured sprigged curtains at the windows. She sat down on the sofa and Liv snuggled up beside her and handed her the gift bag.

"Happy Mother's Day, Mum. Do you miss me?"

Maggie gave a wistful smile.

"Of course. But you're happy, aren't you? That's the best present a mother could wish for."

She opened the gift and gasped. It was a necklace: a fine chain hung with two silver hoops, one inside the other. The outer hoop was engraved with the word *Mum*; the little inner hoop read *Liv*.

"This is how I think of you, Mum, always encircling me, keeping me safe. It's a wonderful comfort, even when we're miles apart."

"It's gorgeous," Maggie whispered, feeling tears gather. "Put it on for me, Liv."

As Liv fastened the chain round Maggie's neck, Dorothy came into the room and put down a tray holding a coffee pot and cups.

"What a lovely Mother's Day scene." She smiled.

Then she frowned, hearing a knock at the door.

It was Nathan, looking very sheepish.

"Sorry to turn up, Gran, but I knew you and Mum would both be here. I'm in a fix."

Maggie hurried out to the hallway.

"Nathan! Is anything wrong?"

"I've just been home," Nathan said anxiously. "Amy and Poppy are both fast asleep. Poor Amy's exhausted so I didn't want to wake her. I'm meant to be cooking her a Mother's Day dinner and there's not a scrap of food in the house. All the supermarkets are closed and I wanted it to be special. Have you anything I could use?"

"Of course." Dorothy laughed. "You know I keep a well-stocked cupboard! Unless . . ." She looked thoughtful. "I wonder if the restaurant could fit us all in?"

Tom looked doubtful.

"No chance," he said. "Mother's Day's a busy night. We only booked a table for three, and we'd need room for seven now, if you counted Poppy in her high chair."

"She wouldn't be well enough anyway," Nathan pointed out. "She's been poorly this week. And Amy's tired out."

"Bless her, she needs a rest," Dorothy said. "Tom, do you think your friend would mind if we cancelled our restaurant reservation?"

"I shouldn't think so. He'd have no trouble filling it again."

"Well, let's all have dinner here! I'll soon rustle something up. Nathan, would you like to go and fetch Amy and Poppy?"

"But . . ." Maggie looked bewildered. "It's Mother's Day. I wanted to treat you!"

Dorothy laughed.

"What does that matter if my family are all here? I can't think of a better Mother's Day present, can you?"

Maggie's looked down at her glamorous dress and grinned.

"No, I can't. I think it's a brilliant idea. Do you have an apron I can borrow, Mum?"

By seven o'clock, everyone was sitting round Dorothy's dining table. The flowers Liv had given her made a beautiful centrepiece.

Maggie and Dorothy had put together a simple but tasty meal of vegetable pasta bake, garlic bread and salad with apple sponge and custard for dessert. Poppy, still a little flushed but happy, sat in her high chair beside Amy.

Maggie smiled warmly at her daughter-in-law.

"How are you feeling now, love?"

"I feel much better after a rest, thank you. Although I think it's going to get worse before it gets better." Smiling, Amy glanced at Nathan, who grinned. "While everyone's here, it seems like a good time for us to tell you. I'm pregnant."

The rest of her words were lost amid the howls of congratulations.

"I only found out this afternoon. It was such a relief to realise that's why I feel so terribly worn out," Amy added.

"It's wonderful news." Dorothy beamed. "But two little ones will be quite a handful. What would you say to having me as a regular helper? I could come as often as you need me."

"That would be fantastic! But wouldn't it be too much for you? Babies are such hard work."

"Nonsense!" Dorothy said with a laugh. "My time is my own, and a bit of hard work is exactly what I need! I'd love to help."

"That's settled, then." Amy grinned widely, eyes shining.

"I'll fetch the dessert," Tom said, getting up. "Give me a hand, will you, Nathan?"

Dorothy surveyed all the happy faces around the table and smiled to herself. Things were indeed changing, and for the better, it seemed.

Soon there would be another addition to the family. What was more, instead of just paying visits to Amy as she did now, she'd help regularly with the babies. A new phase was beginning, and she was very much looking forward to it.

Amy, now feeling refreshed and very excited, was looking forward to it, too. Her little family was growing and the thought of Dorothy's assistance and wisdom was making the immediate future much less daunting. Raising a glass of lemonade to her lips, she gave a little shiver of pleasure.

MAGGIE sat back happily and gazed round at her mother, daughter, daughter-in-law and granddaughter. What was it Nathan's card had said?

Put your feet up.

Well, not one of them had ended up doing that, but what else had it said?

Thanks for being you.

That was what Mother's Day was all about, wasn't it? Mothers and their children, all caring for each other – and discovering how much they were cared for, too!

They might not have put their feet up, but what better way to spend Mother's Day than to have three generations of mothers together – all doing exactly what mothers did best? ■

Illustration by André Leonard.

A Pigeon Pair

by Beatrice Charles.

I
T had started as a throw-away line.

"Let's go travelling when we graduate."

Tom couldn't even remember now which one of the group had suggested it. It had been one of the rare Sunday evenings when all five of the students who shared the large rambling terraced house were home at the same time. As they sat up late talking, all sorts of wild ideas were thrown across the table. From trekking in Peru to backpacking in Thailand; summer camps in America to surfing on Bondi Beach.

It was Ellen, ever the more practical of the housemates, who had suggested an alternative to their daydreams.

"We should give something back," she challenged. "We could approach one of the charities which work abroad. They'd bite our hands off! Five eager volunteers with medical and building qualifications?"

All agreed it was the right thing do rather than waste the year.

Tom volunteered to look into the options. Ellen was right; the skills the five of them could offer would be invaluable to many charities. One project in particular caught his eye which required trained medical staff. Physical help was also required to construct a new medical centre.

As with many ideas embraced in the early hours, in the cold light of day enthusiasm waned. Finally only two of the housemates remained committed to the plan: Tom and Ellen.

The five students were a disparate group. There were two trainee doctors, a mature student reading mechanical engineering, Ellen, who was working hard for her midwifery degree, and Tom, studying quantity surveying. The house they shared was in a run-down area of the city. The furniture was long past its best, the boiler needed gentle handling to keep it operable and the rooms were draughty where the old sash windows no longer fitted. But the five of them had made it their home.

The four guys had met whilst playing hockey for the university team. Ellen had joined them for her final year, responding to an advert for a person to house-share on the student forum's website.

"Remember the golden rule," one of Tom's friends had warned him. "No relationships with housemates. It only leads to complications."

"Don't worry," Tom had replied. "I intend to keep my head down and concentrate on my finals. I don't want any distractions."

But that was before he'd met Ellen. With her golden hair and gentle ways, her determination always to do the right thing, she was difficult to ignore. For seven months he had kept to his resolution – until he heard sobbing one night as he passed by her room. He hesitated on the landing for several minutes before knocking to ask if he could help.

She explained that she had been rereading one of her childhood favourites.

"I always cry when Beth gets sick," she said, waving her copy of "Little Women". "Jo loves her so much . . ."

As her lip quivered Tom proffered another tissue. From that moment their easy friendship as housemates transformed into something much deeper.

That had been two months ago. Now Tom sat alone, supposedly studying but with the textbook open before him unread. Memories of the argument filled his mind. Ever since the phone call from his uncle, everything had changed . . .

There was a loud bang as something hit the window-pane. He stepped outside to the small back yard. A pigeon sat, dazed, on the path.

Beady orange eyes looked warily at him. Tom moved towards the bird but it fluttered clumsily away, its left wing drooping at an awkward angle.

"I won't hurt you," he said quietly, trying to remember what his uncle Jack had taught him in the pigeon loft where, as a child, he had spent many a rainy afternoon.

His uncle's hands as he tended the birds, though rough from years of laying bricks, were gentle. The pigeons relaxed as Jack murmured gently, his voice taking on the gentle resonance of the pigeons.

Settling back on his haunches, Tom clasped his hands together and blew. The noise emitted was a deep sigh. The bird stilled, turning its head to one side. Again Tom made the soft noise, shuffling a little nearer. When he was close enough he reached out and pulled the bird gently to his chest. He continued to murmur words of reassurance while he examined the damaged wing.

"You need to stay a while," he said.

"THEY can find their way home over hundreds of miles," Uncle Jack said. "If they were my birds, I'd never let them fly away!" Tom protested.

"You have to let them fly," his uncle said, ruffling the boy's hair. "They'll come back – they're very determined. And brave. Some pigeons won medals during the war, taking messages behind enemy lines."

"Do they always return?"

"Mine always have. Very rarely a bird will choose to live somewhere else. Look at this little one here." He placed a beautiful white dove with grey flecks along her wings carefully into Tom's hands. Tom could feel the tiny heart beating.

"This little hen turned up three years ago. Beautiful, isn't she? Poor thing was way off course. She belonged to a fancier in Falkirk."

"You kept her?"

"I offered to send her home but her owner said as she wanted to stay, I should keep her. I call her Little Morag, but don't let your aunt know."

The old man winked and Tom grinned at the thought of his auntie Morag's indignation if she learned her husband had named a bird after her.

Taking the dove from the child, Jack placed her back on the ledge. Another bird with fluffy feathers on its feet and a large fanned tail flew across, bobbing its head up and down and turning in circles around her. It seemed as though he was inspecting Little Morag to make sure she had not been harmed.

"I call this fussy fellow Little Jack. Pigeons stay together for life. She left her home loft to be here with him. And this Little Jack would no more leave his Morag than I could be apart from your auntie."

* * * *

With no children of their own, his uncle and aunt had adopted Tom after his parents died in a car accident. It couldn't have been easy for them at their age, adjusting to life with a sorrowing six-year-old boy, but they had surrounded him with love, and in time, with their help, he overcame his grief.

Jack had telephoned yesterday to tell him Morag had fallen. Nothing broken, but this was the second fall she'd had in the last month. It served as a reminder that they were growing increasingly frail.

Tom felt torn between his obligation to them and his desire to be with Ellen. If only he could persuade her to change her mind and find a job at home.

He turned his thoughts back to the fragile creature he held in his hands. He carried it into the kitchen just as the front door opened and Ellen returned home.

At the sight of Tom nursing the wounded pigeon, she rushed forward to help.

"Poor thing!" she said as Tom explained what had happened. "What can I do to help?"

"In my bedroom there's a plastic crate. Will you empty it out and tear up newspaper to make a bed? And we need something to hold water. Not a saucer, it's too shallow. Some rice and barley from the cupboard will do until we can buy some wild bird seed."

Over the next two weeks Tom and Ellen nursed the wounded bird together. They avoided speaking about the future, but focused their attention firmly on the tiny living being which needed their care.

* * * *

Finally the day came to set the pigeon free. Tom removed the lid from the crate. The bird lifted its head and sunlight reflected from the iridescent green and purple feathers at its neck.

After a few practice swipes of its wings the pigeon rose up above the rooftop. Turning in ever widening circles above them, it ascended higher and then flew steadily south.

Ellen gazed skyward even though the pigeon had long since flown from view. Tom stood behind her.

"I wonder if it will find its way home?"

"Sometimes it's hard to let go." Tom placed his arms on her shoulders.

She nodded and he knew she was close to tears.

"Ellen, when you qualify . . ."

She turned to face him.

"I don't want to leave you – I love you. But they're relying on me, Tom. I have to take up my placement at the mission hospital."

"I know. I've been thinking about this, and I remembered something my uncle once told me about making choices. I was being selfish. I was wrong to try to persuade you not to go."

"But what about you? What will you do?"

"As soon as the exams are over I'll go home. My uncle and aunt were there when I needed them and I won't let them down now. I'll take over the family building firm so Jack can retire and look after Morag. When the year is over, will you return, Ellen? Will you promise to come home to me?"

As she threw her arms around his neck, he knew with certainty that she would. ▪

Plant Predictors

ONE way of predicting the weather that's been used for centuries is to notice the behaviour of plants.

Pine cones are a well-known natural barometer. They open up when it's dry and close when it's going to rain. Seaweed also responds to moisture in the air, when it expands and feels damp. In dry conditions it shrivels and feels dry to the touch. It's easier to use seaweed for forecasting after any early morning dew has evaporated!

Some flowers also forecast rain by closing up, opening fully when it's dry again. Daisies and dandelions both do this, but the little red flowers of the scarlet pimpernel are perhaps best known for their forecasting abilities. So responsive is the flower that it was once known as the "poor man's weatherglass".

The leaves of some trees such as oak, poplar, lime and sycamore also react to moisture in the atmosphere. The stalks become softer, causing the leaves to turn over and show their undersides. This indicates that rain may not be far away.

If rain is on the way you might be able to smell it before you see it! Rain is a feature of low pressure in the atmosphere, while fine, sunny weather is a feature of high pressure. The delicate scent of many plants and flowers can be trapped at lower levels by high pressure. As the pressure lessens, the scent travels higher, so if you can smell the flowers in your garden when you couldn't before, there may be a shower on the way!

Illustration by Ruth Blair.

Once Bitten . . .

by Susan Blackburn.

So that's the new neighbour, Lauren thought as she gazed listlessly through the kitchen window, drinking yet another mug of tea. He was peering over the fence that divided their two back gardens. She could clearly see the expression of disbelief on his handsome face as he surveyed the jungle that was hers.

And it was a jungle, Lauren had to admit, looking at it for the first time through somebody else's eyes. She and Carl had had such plans for it when they'd bought this, their first home. It had been wonderfully cheap as it needed such a lot of work, but they had both been excited by the challenge.

They'd concentrated on the house first, looking forward to sorting the garden at their leisure.

Then, just before their wedding, Carl had broken off the engagement. It turned out that backpacking around Australia appealed to him more than married life.

"It's not you. It's me, Lauren," he'd said, delivering the awful cliché awkwardly one evening, out of the blue.

In shock, she couldn't face the hassle of selling the house. By using her savings and with some help from her parents, who wanted to do all they could to support their distraught daughter, she bought Carl out and took over the mortgage.

But the last thing on her mind had been the garden. It was enough of a struggle getting up each morning, when all she really wanted to do was pull the duvet over her head.

Looking more closely now at the garden as she sipped her tea, Lauren could see, despite the tangled mess, bulbs peeping through and shoots appearing on some of the surviving shrubs. Spring. A time of new growth and new life.

The sun suddenly came out and danced through the trees bordering the back fence, just as it had in those first months after they'd bought the house.

Now, as the sun warmed her face through the window, she realised she'd lost her own enthusiasm. But no more, Lauren thought, a surge of unexpected energy sweeping through her.

Pulling on jeans and a sweater and her stoutest shoes, she extracted from the bookcase the file in which they'd put the plans. Carl's plans, to be honest. He had been the gardener; she would have been the willing assistant.

SHE couldn't do this! She threw the file back in the bookcase, dashing away the treacherous tears that still caught her out. Rushing upstairs, she was just about to disappear under the duvet when the doorbell rang.

She ignored it. It rang again. Flinging some water on her tear-stained face, she trudged downstairs.

It was her new neighbour.

"Hi, I'm Gordon. I've just moved in next door. Well, not just, I've been there a fair while, actually. Thought I'd pop round and introduce myself." He stuck out his hand. "Are you OK?" he added, frowning.

How peculiar, Lauren thought crossly. She would never have thought of "popping round" to introduce herself to a total stranger, even if it was a new neighbour. It should be a gradual "getting to know you" over the garden fence, or a polite hello in the driveway.

She half-heartedly took the hand Gordon offered her and found her own squeezed tightly as he shook it. At least he didn't have one of those horrid limp handshakes. As her eyes travelled upwards she realised he was very tall, with blond hair falling forward to just above the most dazzling green eyes she'd ever seen.

"Lauren. I'm fine; nice to meet you," she burbled. "Sorry, I've got something on the stove. Hope you settle in well."

And she shut the door.

* * * *

Well, that was rude, she thought to herself. But she was bemused at the feelings that had been unleashed by that hand-clasp and by looking into those green eyes. For heaven's sake, whatever had come over her? She was off men for life. Absolutely and categorically!

Now she was going to be embarrassed if she saw him, she thought furiously. Besides, she had been quite happy wallowing.

Wallowing. That was what she'd been doing, Lauren admitted, suddenly ashamed. Well, no more! She pulled the gardening file from the bookcase.

THE following Saturday Lauren was aware of Gordon watching her with interest over the garden fence as she got hotter and hotter, trying to clear some of the jungle.

"Hi, there," he called. "Lovely afternoon! I'm just having a glass of iced tea. Would you care to join me?"

She was grateful at the thought. She was thirsty and exhausted.

"No, thank you," she found herself replying suddenly, the cool tone a huge contrast to her hot person. "Must get on."

"Fine," he said.

She suspected he was making a great play of serving his drink to annoy her. She could hear the chink of the ice cubes, then the glug of the iced tea as he poured it. She imagined him drinking the refreshing liquid . . .

She found herself at the fence. She might have sworn off men, but it was only a glass of iced tea!

"Perhaps I will, thank you," she said diffidently.

He looked up from his newspaper.

"Come on round," he said, beaming a huge smile that lit up those amazing green eyes.

∗   ∗   ∗   ∗

Sipping her tea, she looked around his garden. It was beautifully laid out. She realised Gordon was speaking.

"I have a rotavator. That bit you were digging looks like it could do with it."

She glanced up at him and as their eyes met she found it difficult to look away.

Mentally she shook herself. This was ridiculous – she'd only just met the man. Still, she really could do with some help with her jungle.

"If you're sure, that would be brilliant." She was flustered and her voice came out in an infuriating squeak. "Your garden looks good," she rushed on, really for something to say. Although, it actually did look wonderful. "Have you done all this since you moved in?"

"Pretty much," Gordon said. "Although, to be fair, it wasn't too bad. It just needed a bit of redesigning and shaping."

"You designed this?"

Now Lauren really took in what she was looking at. Curved pathways, a pond, shaped flower-beds. The overall effect was stunning.

"Yep. Of course, a lot of it was here already. All the spring bulbs, the early flowering shrubs."

"Is gardening your main interest, then?" Lauren asked.

Gordon laughed.

"It should be. I'm a landscape gardener."

Lauren couldn't help but laugh.

"Ah. That would explain the rotavator."

Over another cup of tea Lauren found herself, much to her surprise, telling Gordon about her break-up with Carl.

"My ex did something rather similar," Gordon said quietly. "In the end her job overseas carried more glamour, apparently, than being married to a landscape gardener."

The woman must have been mad, Lauren thought, then pulled herself up sharply. Don't go there, she warned herself.

"Look, Lauren." Gordon was speaking again. "I'm certainly not looking to get involved with anybody again any time soon. But the fact is, we're neighbours, you have a jungle of a garden and I've got the knowledge to help you." He held out his hand. "Deal?"

"Deal," she said.

Once again her treacherous body let her down at his touch. And she felt such a shaft of regret on hearing him state he didn't want to get involved with anyone any time soon, she could hardly bear it.

I T was a perfect late summer's day. Lauren was sitting in the little arbour Gordon had built for her, surrounded by the sweet scent of the roses growing around it. A bottle of chilled wine and two glasses were on the table in front of her.

"Hi." Gordon came up behind her, bent forward and kissed her.

"Hi, yourself," she said.

She was still unable to believe what had happened over the last few months as they'd transformed her garden. Having such fun together; a gradual thawing of distrust and fear on both sides; a casual supper together after a hard day's gardening.

Then the first tentative kiss, both still not sure this was a sensible road to venture down.

"I think I first loved you when you opened your door and I saw that little tear-stained face staring up at me," Gordon had confessed afterwards.

"It was when you shook my hand and I looked up into your eyes," Lauren had told him in turn. "It all felt so right. But I didn't dare admit how I felt, either."

Gordon poured the wine into the glasses.

"Here's to gardens," he said, handing her one of them.

"And to a certain gardener." She laughed.

It was early days but, just as a new garden flourishes and grows, Lauren was pretty sure the first tender shoots of their love would do the same. ▨

Illustration by Kirk Houston/Thinkstockphotos.

A Spring In Her Step

by Rebecca Mansell.

WHEN I was a little girl, Cherry, my adorable puppy, was always by my side. My brother and I used to play hide and seek all the time because we were fortunate to live in a big, old farmhouse with plenty of places to conceal our small bodies from prying eyes.

"Look and listen for Cherry, and that's where you'll find Ellie," my mother used to tell Frank.

Of course, Cherry would inevitably give away my hiding place by a small, excited yap or an over-exuberant scuffling sound when she tried to leap on to my lap.

Then, when Frank found me, Cherry would join in by eagerly chasing us down the hallway as we ran happily into our mother's arms.

"You'll always lose this game," my mother often said, kissing my forehead affectionately, "with your little poodle as your constant shadow."

I never really did understand why my mother referred to Cherry as a poodle, because she was a black Labrador. Yet, funnily enough, when my mother said the word "poodle" Cherry used to go to her and sit at her feet, tilting her head to one side enquiringly.

Cherry grew into a beautiful, energetic dog. She never tired of exploring, constantly dashing through bushes and racing elatedly around trees.

I loved her so very much. She was my best friend.

When she died, at the grand old age of seventeen, a part of me disappeared with her. Being in my early twenties didn't prevent the grief of losing her from overwhelming me. I was inconsolable.

"Why don't you get another dog?" Frank suggested helpfully, to which I only shook my head miserably.

Cherry was irreplaceable.

I'm sure one of the reasons why I fell in love with Adrian was because he loved animals as much as I did. We met at a lecture I was giving on pet therapy at the local university.

"I'm a vet," he said to me afterwards. "My name is Adrian."

I smiled at his simple introduction, taking note of his scruffy dark brown hair and lopsided grin.

"I'm a psychologist, as you'll have gathered, and my name is Ellen."

He shook my hand firmly.

"How about dinner?"

"It's only eleven o'clock."

"Brunch, then?"

"OK."

I decided to be spontaneous and go out with a complete stranger, and it was a decision I never regretted. Adrian even proposed to me that day. Of course, I said no.

I said yes the next day, instead.

Our whirlwind romance culminated in a beautiful wedding overflowing with love and laughter. I was the luckiest girl alive. Except something was missing, and it was obvious what that was.

OUR children grew up and flew the nest and Adrian and I settled into a new routine.

"We should have had a dog," Adrian said to me one day when I was gazing forlornly at the frosted grass outside and the grey sky. I was sure it was going to snow. It seemed darker than normal, the sun unable to squeeze through the formidable, heavy clouds.

Glancing at Adrian, I saw his eyes were serious.

"Perhaps," I answered, trying to smile. "It would have been good for the children."

"And good for you, too."

I nodded my head, but secretly I didn't agree. The times I'd shared with Cherry still occupied a part of my heart I was sure another dog could never fill.

"I worry you'll be lonely now."

"I have plenty to occupy me," I argued. "I still have a few clients to help, and the garden always keeps me busy."

Adrian leaned behind me to flick on the kettle, then turned to look at me again, his brow furrowed with concern, and I wrapped my arms around his neck, kissing him softly on the lips.

"Don't worry about me. I'm happy with just you in my life. I was before the children arrived, and I will be now."

Adrian gave me an affectionate hug back.

"I forgot to tell you. We have a yellow Labrador at the surgery. She's about to give birth – I reckon the pups will be adorable."

He'd done this a lot over the years: tried to tempt me with all sorts of waifs and strays that came into the surgery. One time he'd even persuaded me to take a look at a homeless springer spaniel who'd been abandoned. Friendly and affectionate though the dog was, I'd decided that he'd be far too boisterous and excitable to train. Not to mention his separation anxiety issues. Who would look after him when we weren't home? Who would take him for long walks every day?

"I'm sure they'll be absolutely lovely, and dog lovers will be falling over themselves to have one."

"*You're* a dog lover," Adrian said, kissing me gently on the nose. "With more compassion than most."

"I'm just me." I shrugged. "The woman you've been married to for thirty years."

"And the woman I adore more each and every day."

Yes, I was very fortunate to have met Adrian all those years ago.

Later that day, when I was alone again, I thought about his words. Would a dog have added something special to our little world? Perhaps I had been selfish in my desire to keep my memories of Cherry to myself. Over the years I'd seen many families out walking with their dogs and the familiar yearning, which had once been so intense, had faded as time went by. I had my children to care for and my husband. What more did I need?

* * * *

The postman was very late that day. Perhaps the weather had hindered his round. The rain pounding against the window made me think it probably wasn't going to snow after all. The house was dark, but I didn't want to put a light on for that seemed to signal the end of the day and Adrian wasn't due home for several more hours.

A feeling of desolation swept over me. It was very quiet. I wasn't used to this. I was used to the children coming home from school, and then, when they did, they'd sit in the kitchen and tell me all about their day, recounting their adventures, filling me in on their friends' latest exploits (which they never played a part in, they assured me) and asking me for help with their homework. The children, Adrian and my hectic work schedule had occupied all my time.

An insistent voice confirmed that I hadn't been entirely honest with my husband earlier. I *was* lonely.

Surely my experience as a psychologist could help me with this? After all, I had treated so many people who were isolated as a result of their emotional difficulties and their fears. And I wasn't afraid, not of anything.

The sound of the post falling on to the mat shook me from my reverie. As I bent to pick it up, a brightly coloured flyer slipped from my grasp and slithered to the floor. I eyed it suspiciously. Probably a company trying to tempt me into buying their latest product or service. Sighing, I reached down for it . . . and let out a tiny gasp. The picture on the front looked just like Cherry!

Sparkle needs care and attention and most of all love. Can you help?

I frowned. Was this an organisation needing homes for abandoned pets? I didn't have the time for that. Even so, I nursed a mug of coffee and read the leaflet further.

Heartfield takes care of animals that have been neglected and mistreated by providing them with a supportive environment devoted to their needs. Here at Heartfield, we lavish our animals with love and attention and help them to learn to trust humans again.

We are a small voluntary organisation but with an abundance of compassion and kindness to share.

If you have a big heart and you love all creatures great and small, then join us in our pursuit of making our animals feel loved and wanted.

Ring us today.

My fingers inched towards my mobile phone, sitting on the table. There was something about the leaflet that appealed to me. I had reservations, of course. Did I really have the time and commitment to offer? Just because the dog looked like Cherry . . .

"More compassion than most." Adrian's words echoed in my head, and I smiled.

Was I ready to help animals in need?

Many years ago I'd decided to be spontaneous and go on a date with a man

I'd never met before, and the result had been a life filled with love and happiness.

Perhaps it was time to give something back . . .

HEARTFIELD? Yes, I've heard of it. They regularly bring animals to us for inspection." My husband was unable to conceal the delight in his eyes. "I'm so happy you've done this."

"You are?" I gazed back at him. "I'm not sure I can be much help, though," I said thoughtfully. "Many of their dogs and cats are so frightened and wary. After the induction I had an hour with a dog called Ben, a beagle, and he spent most of it whimpering in my arms."

Adrian gave me a supportive hug.

"I can assure you, you will be giving those animals comfort and reassurance that they aren't used to. It'll be so rewarding for you. That's what makes me so happy. Just you wait and see."

Adrian had rarely been wrong about anything in the 30 years I'd known him. Before long, Sophie, a springer spaniel, wagged her tail frantically whenever she saw me. Tufty the Persian cat leaped on my lap for me to stroke her long, soft fur whenever we stopped for a coffee and a chat, and a beautiful Siberian husky with amazing blue eyes allowed only me to feed her.

And Ben wanted me to walk him every day.

As the animals grew in confidence, so did I. I had a spring in my step that I didn't have before.

*   *   *   *

"You were right," I said to Adrian after a particularly busy day. "I love it."

"I knew you would." He beamed back at me. "You have so much love to give."

"And plenty left over for you." I laughed, pecking him on the cheek as I rose to take his dinner plate to the sink. "Lots and lots."

"And for a new member of the family?"

I had my back to him as he spoke and I stopped, staring out the window. The daffodils were beginning to bud and a robin and a thrush were on the bird table, shouting at each other. Spring was just around the corner. A new beginning.

"Perhaps," I said cautiously. "Maybe."

Every morning I felt a new-found vitality and vigour that I used to feel when I was a child. Jumping out of bed, and after a very light breakfast, I shrugged on my tracksuit bottoms and a warm fleece and went for a jog along the beach. I loved the fresh, revitalising breeze as I dodged the waves.

Adrian was always contentedly slumbering away when I left and I was careful not to disturb him. He worked hard, after all. So did I, but if anything,

Maypole Dancers

WHAT a happy sight to see,
When little children skip with glee
Round a maypole, ribboned bright,
A simple scene of sheer delight.
Round and round and round they go
How happily they ebb and flow;
They prance and dance in their display,
To herald in the month of May.
         – Brian H. Gent.

I felt more energy than ever before.

When I got home I'd find my husband staring blearily into his coffee and yawning.

"Perhaps I need fresh air in my lungs, too."

I chuckled.

"It would do you good."

"I think I'm more of a walker than a runner," he said in response.

"Yes, slowcoach!" I laughed, drinking fresh orange juice.

"Hey, I can keep up with you!" Adrian caught me in a warm embrace. "I'll prove it to you one day."

"I look forward to that," I murmured. "I really do."

THE following day, I went for my run along the beach and thought about the tiny kittens that had been brought into Heartfield the night before. They'd been abandoned at a roadside. I couldn't imagine anyone doing that. They mewed constantly, but by the time I left, we'd fed them and they were curled up all together with a teddy bear we'd found to bring them comfort. All they really needed was love.

It was a beautiful morning. The sun was just beginning to rise but there was warmth in the breeze and the sea was a serene turquoise colour.

Seagulls overhead sounded almost sorrowful. I didn't feel that way any more. The children were coming home next weekend and I couldn't wait to see them. And if something was still missing, well, I didn't want to admit to myself what it might be . . .

Up ahead I could see a tiny speck in the distance. I squinted and it became two specks.

I frowned. Normally I was alone on the beach at this hour. I was here to jog, get some fresh air, so I sped along.

Strangely enough, the two specks seemed to be running, too. Perhaps they were training for the local marathon in the summer.

They were getting closer and I frowned. One was much faster than the other, and smaller. Before I knew it, a yellow Labrador puppy leaped eagerly into my arms and I fell to the sand, rolling around with the furry, adorable animal which licked my face enthusiastically.

"What the . . .?" I gasped as I sat up and peered at a pair of scruffy trainers. They looked familiar, though I hadn't seen them for a while.

"Adrian!"

He was kitted out in a tracksuit, a little ill fitting, but somehow he managed to look the part.

"What are you doing?"

"Adding a bit more joy to your life."

The puppy yapped at me excitedly and then jumped into my arms again. I giggled as we tumbled around on the sand.

"I think he likes you." Adrian crouched down next to us. "His name is Jake."

"Jake." I gazed into the dog's chocolate brown eyes. "He's gorgeous."

"He needs a new home – with us. I thought it was time."

I stood up slowly, gazing out to sea with Jake trying to climb up my leg.

"I know he'll never replace Cherry," Adrian said, slipping an arm around my waist. "But what do you think?"

I turned to look at my husband.

"I think thirty years ago I made the right decision when I went out with you."

"And now?"

I smiled.

"You've made the right decision, too."

"I'm so glad." Adrian kissed me gently as the puppy suddenly let out an exuberant bark. "But is it OK if we go out walking with the dog rather than jogging? The run across the beach at this early hour nearly killed me!"

"I thought you said you could keep up?" I teased him, running ahead with Jake close at my heels. "Come on, let's show Jake his new home!"

And I raced ahead, with the love of my life close behind me and my new puppy bounding ahead.

I said goodbye to loneliness that day. ■

Aberystwyth, Wales

THE graceful, sweeping seafront of Aberystwyth is a favourite with visitors and locals alike. If you walk the full length of the 2,000-metre promenade you'll pass various sights and landmarks – from the harbour and marina in the south to the busy main beach and Constitution Hill at the northern end.

You might notice the unusual flags flying along the promenade while you're there. They do not represent major powers, but are a selection of the minority nations and regions of Europe which have their own unique languages. The flags are there as a sign of support and friendship from a country which is very proud of its own Welsh language.

You'll also find a children's paddling pool and traditional seaside entertainment along the promenade in the summer season. Don't forget to check out the bandstand, too, which is a popular venue for local bands, performers and choirs. ◼

Two Weeks In Annecy

by Pauline Bradbury.

I T'S only two weeks in France." Sally lifted the pizza out of the oven and dumped it on the kitchen table.

"I know, Sal." Rob could see that she was getting impatient and it was going to spoil the evening. "It's just, anything can happen in two weeks," he finished lamely. After all, he could hardly explain that he was feeling left out.

"Anything or nothing at all," Sally told him. "Come on, let's eat."

On the surface the evening passed pleasantly. They sat holding hands in companionable silence watching a thriller on TV, and when Rob got up to go, he decided it best not to mention the subject again, although Sally could feel it between them. They had been an item for a long time.

Too long, Sally thought later, pushing the misgivings she had been feeling for some time to the back of her mind. Time apart will do us good.

Running down the stairs the next morning, she thought for the umpteenth time how lucky she was to have a job that she loved and a boss that she liked and admired. Debbie Lodge had built up the Daisy Chain until it was the most popular florist in town. When Sally had first been offered a job there, she had been unsure of herself, but she had soon discovered an unsuspected flair. Now she rented the flat above the shop, with Debbie telling her that she couldn't manage without her. Life was good.

Then, a few weeks ago, Debbie had shown her trust in Sally even further.

"I was wondering," she said one morning while they were awaiting their delivery of fresh flowers, "whether you feel capable of taking over from me whilst I take my mum to France next month? Just for two weeks, while I settle her into the holiday flat she's renting."

Sally swung round in astonishment, but knew what her answer would be without stopping to think.

"If she hadn't had that hip operation I wouldn't bother, because she's used to travelling on her own. But I'd feel happier to be with her, you know, crossing Paris and changing trains," Debbie explained.

"Yes, of course," Sally assured her, more than happy to pick up the challenge.

But a week ago something unexpected happened. Debbie went down with shingles.

"There's no way I can go," she reported over the phone. "But I may just be able to keep the shop going, with the help of the two part-timers."

"And me, of course," Sally interrupted.

"I have another plan for you," Debbie went on. "Is your passport up to date?"

This was what Rob wasn't happy about – Sally stepping in and accompanying Debbie's mother to Annecy

Illustration by Philip Crabb/Thinkstockphotos.

and, Sally suspected, using up two weeks of her own holiday leave to do so.

"It still leaves me two weeks to go away with Rob later on," Sally told herself as she began opening up for the day. "And this time next week . . ."

*   *   *   *

"This time last week," Sally mused to herself, as she lay in one of the twin beds in the apartment which Sandra Lodge had rented for six months, "I hadn't realised how two train journeys and a new friend could change life so rapidly."

Her mind flitted through the happy images of the journey to Annecy. Sandra had turned out to be a feisty older version of her daughter, so that by the time they stepped out of the air-conditioned train into the warmth of an Annecy evening they were firm friends.

Sally stretched contentedly, then felt guilty when she realised that in all the excitement she had hardly given poor Rob a thought.

Sandra stirred in the other bed.

"Oh, you're awake, Sally." She smiled. "Will we explore before it gets too hot?"

Annecy was a magical little town with canals running through its centre, alongside which were numerous cafés and shops. And the turquoise lake, with trees shading the near edge and mountains rising all round its far sides, was so beautiful, so romantic. Annecy was enchanting; Sally was enchanted.

Later Sandra suggested they take an evening stroll down to the lakeside, and in a little clearing among the trees, overhung with coloured lanterns, was a

59

small concrete circle on which a crowd of people were dancing to the music from an accordion and a keyboard, helped along by a husky-voiced singer. The whole effect was charming and unexpected.

"Oh, I love dancing!" Sandra exclaimed, to Sally's astonishment. "It would be a good chance to try out my new hip. Do you think I could find a partner?"

So, while Sally hung shyly at the back of the onlookers, Sandra pushed herself forward and the next moment was being led on to the dance floor by a somewhat portly French gentleman in impeccable white shirt and trousers. Sally watched in amazement.

Not long after that she found herself being tapped on the shoulder by a good-looking guy in navy shorts and a bright blue shirt.

"*Dansez avec moi?*" he asked hesitatingly.

"I'm sorry, I'm not very good at French," Sally said inconsequentially.

"Thank goodness," he replied in an unmistakable English accent. "I'm no good at all, but would you like to dance?"

"Well, I'm not very good at dancing, either," Sally told him apologetically.

"We can try," he suggested coaxingly. "I only do a sort of manly shuffle."

Sally giggled.

"We'll have a go," she agreed.

Whether it was the cheerful and rhythmic tune, or the gusto of their fellow dancers, they managed quite creditably, and Sally found herself clapping enthusiastically at the end of the dance.

She remembered Sandra.

"I'm supposed to be looking after somebody," she said guiltily, looking round the throng.

"If it's the lady you were with, I don't think you need worry." He nodded to one side where Sandra was cheerfully chatting to her partner, obviously waiting for the music to begin again.

"Her hip must be holding up," Sally remarked, and went on to explain how she came to be in Annecy. "A companion for two weeks," she said. "Although Sandra doesn't really need looking after, so it's more of a holiday."

"Lucky you." He smiled. "I'm camping just outside town. A holiday on a very tight budget before I go back to the real world."

"TOBY TEMPLETON," Sandra mused that evening after Toby had escorted them home. "That name has a nice wholesome ring to it."

"As has Albert Joubert of the elegant white outfit," Sally teased. "And don't forget I'm spoken for."

"Hmm," Sandra replied, gazing at Sally's left hand. "I don't see any ring."

"We don't need rings nowadays," Sally replied lightly.

But the next day she realised that a ring on her finger would have sent out the appropriate message to Toby, who turned up just as they got back from breakfast at the *boulangerie* across the road.

"Oh, good," Sandra said. "You two can stroll down to the market for me."

The street market was easy to find and very busy, with what seemed like all the housewives in Annecy there, eager to strike a bargain.

Suddenly Toby reached for Sally's hand.

"We might lose each other amongst this throng," was his excuse.

"We might," Sally agreed, feeling uneasy, and resolving to tell him about Rob at the first opportunity.

Hand in hand they strolled past the rows of stalls, whose orange umbrellas vied with the vibrant mix of peaches, plums, tomatoes and peppers arranged decoratively beneath. It was a glory of colour.

"Wow!" Toby exclaimed. "Easy to eat healthily here."

"Totally," Sally agreed, trying to ignore the feelings his firm clasp gave her.

They delivered their purchases back to Sandra, who suggested they went off sightseeing.

"Then you're welcome to join us for supper, Toby." She smiled, dismissing them both with a wave of her hand.

Now, Sally thought as they walked off, is the moment to set the record straight.

"Look, Toby," she began. "I hope it doesn't seem to you as if Sandra is throwing us together, because I have a boyfriend back home. It sounds awfully big-headed to assume you might be interested in me like that," she went on, red with embarrassment, "but I don't want you to get mixed messages."

Toby's brown eyes met her blue ones steadily.

"I can't say I'm not disappointed," he told her honestly. "Meeting you like that seemed too good to be true." He hesitated. "We can still enjoy each other's company, can't we? As friends?"

"Of course." Sally tried not to sound as enthusiastic as she felt. After all, it would be easy to be friends with Toby now she had made the situation clear.

✳   ✳   ✳   ✳

"Your time here is so short, Sally," Sandra said as they were going to bed. "Make the most of it."

Making the most of it consisted of wandering the streets with Toby, sipping coffee at pavement cafés, buying baguettes for lunch and picnicking by the lake. None of which cost much money, which was just as well as Sally discovered that Toby was doing this holiday on a shoestring because he was a student.

"A mature student," he explained. "I suddenly decided to change my life around, and now . . ." He hesitated.

"Now?" Sally prompted.

"Well, I've been a theological student," he finished. "Soon I will be ordained. But I'm really just an ordinary guy underneath."

Privately Sally was beginning to feel that he was anything but ordinary. He was becoming far too intriguing for her peace of mind. She was trying to suppress those feelings, but it would do no harm to encourage him to talk about his studies and aims, which she found very interesting. And she told him so.

"That's a relief," he confided, "Because it's a put-off to most girls."

"I'm not most girls," she retorted quickly, then was appalled at how rude that sounded. "Sorry," she apologised hastily. "That didn't come out right."

"No, you're not most girls," Toby agreed. "I knew that as soon as I saw you."

We're on dangerous ground here, Sally warned herself, trying to ignore the tug of tension and attraction which had suddenly materialised between them.

"So, what shall we do next?" she asked brightly. "Walk up to the cathedral?"

The days passed in this heady mix of relaxing warmth and colourful surroundings. England and Rob seemed far away. Toby and Sandra and even Monsieur Joubert, who often joined them for supper, seemed much more real.

"We haven't been on a steamer trip round the lake yet," Toby told her on her last day. "Let's do that."

It was a wonderful climax to her holiday. The views were breathtaking. Craggy mountains with still higher peaks behind, fairytale *châteaux* perched on impossible outcrops, small villages nestling on narrow strips of flat land on the shores. Sally was spellbound.

"I've stored it all up in my mind," she told Toby as they walked homewards. "So I can remember it always."

They had just reached the so-called Lovers' Bridge when Toby turned to her and determinedly pulled her to him.

"I apologise in advance for this," he murmured, his face so close that Sally could see a mischievous gleam in his eyes, and then he kissed her. When he straightened up, the mischievous look had gone and she saw regret.

"Apology accepted," Sally managed to stammer lightly, even though in that moment her world had turned upside-down.

She managed to push her tumultuous feelings to the back of her mind for the rest of the day, concentrating on getting ready for the next morning.

Even though it was very early, Toby was waiting at the station the next morning and, very surprisingly, Monsieur Joubert was there, too. He kissed her hand in farewell, which gave Toby the chance to do the same, and as he did so Toby pushed a small box into her hand and closed her fingers round it.

"I hope I'm not going to cry!" Sally laughed as she climbed into the train.

"Of course you're not," Sandra told her, brisk as ever. "Thank you for your company and all your help, and *bon voyage*."

The tears came after Sally sat down, because inside Toby's box was a delicate old ring – an aquamarine in a neat silver setting which fitted perfectly on her finger. She would wear it always, she told herself forlornly.

It was the message in Toby's sprawling handwriting that brought the tears.

This is to help you remember the colour of the lake which you loved so much, and to wish you every happiness in your future life.

It was a different Sally on the return journey. One who needed to come to grips with her kaleidoscope of emotions. By the time she reached Paris, she knew she must break off her relationship with Rob. Not only because it had become stale, but because she realised that it had never produced any of the depth of feeling that should have been there in the first place. It had been a safe and cosy relationship, but that wasn't enough. Toby's kiss had revealed that.

Even though her chance with Toby had gone, she must make Rob accept her decision.

"Rob," she muttered, suddenly realising that she hadn't had a text from him for two days and hadn't even wondered why.

Are you OK? she texted now.

It wasn't until she reached her flat that night that she had the answer. He'd had an accident on his bike and had broken his left wrist and right shoulder.

So much for my decision, she thought wryly as she replied that she would pick him up from hospital the next day. That will have to wait.

I F it ever happened at all, Sally thought a few weeks later. A few weeks of being Rob's nursemaid had suppressed all her see-sawing emotions, so that she and Rob were back in the groove again as if nothing had happened.

Annecy had been and gone. All that was left were her memories, the precious ring, and a very grateful Debbie who was big with plans for opening another shop and putting Sally in charge. Life was pressured and busy.

But quite pleasant, Sally acknowledged to herself. If this was what the rest of her life turned out to be like then it wouldn't be so bad after all, she thought as she stuffed washing in the machine after a busy day at the shop.

"A relationship is bound to settle down," she told herself, "with emotional highs giving way to a more contented existence. I may even say yes next time Rob hints about marriage." She smiled, picturing Rob's delighted face.

After six weeks the plaster was taken off and Rob was back at work full time, but his shoulder was not doing so well.

"I've got to have physio," he told Sally, hugging her as she got in from the Daisy Chain one evening. "Then I shall be as good as new."

The physio seemed to work straight away. At once Rob was more positive.

"She's very good," he told Sally after a few sessions. "Knows what's what. Lili, I mean."

"Lily?" Sally was busy serving the pasta.

"She's Chinese. It's pronounced Lee-lee," Rob corrected her.

"Lily. Same difference," Sally replied cheerfully, ladling the sauce over their plates. "I'm glad you're getting there, Rob, because I'm going to be so busy in the next few weeks with the new shop that you'll have to fend for yourself."

And so she was. It was all so stimulating and exciting. Debbie had asked her to help plan and oversee the alterations to the small shop near St Andrew's Church, choose the décor and decide on the first consignment of flowers.

"I have complete trust in your abilities," Debbie had told her after returning from a quick trip to Annecy. "It's all yours. Mum sent her love. She's got less than a month there now so is making the most of it."

"Does she still see Monsieur Joubert?" Sally couldn't resist asking.

"Albert?" Debbie smiled. "He's a bit of a fixture in Mum's life at the moment."

There was no point in mentioning Toby's name, Sally thought. He had intended hitchhiking home the day after she left.

*   *   *   *

Sally failed to see any significance over the next few weeks about Rob's movements. He seemed to have picked up the threads of his social life with his mates, was unfailingly kind and grateful when she visited, and his shoulder was improving.

"Though it may take months to get the full strength back," he told her one day when she had done a supermarket shop and was filling his fridge.

"Well, we can wait," Sally said positively. "Bound to get there in the end."

He didn't answer, and as her back was turned to him, she didn't see the agonised look flash over his face at her use of the word "we".

In the end, it was quite by chance that she found out. She had nipped out in the lunch hour to choose a card for a friend.

"Back in ten," she had called to Debbie.

And in ten minutes she was indeed back. But it felt more like ten hours, for she had seen them through the window of the bookshop: Rob and a petite dark-haired girl, queuing at the newly opened coffee bar inside, hand in hand.

"I need half an hour," she told Debbie, making for the stairs up to her flat.

Debbie had been very good about it in her briskly sympathetic way, and instead of giving her time off, had kept Sally so busy that she had no time for moping or bitterness, and each night she dropped off to sleep without any of the painful "what if" scenarios flooding her mind.

"DEBBIE doesn't do hand-holding." Sally smiled wryly to herself as she stood in Daisy Chain Two, wondering if she had got the shelving at the back of the shop exactly right. "But I don't think that would have done me much good anyway."

It was weeks later and the opening of Daisy Chain Two was imminent. The shop looked good. Sally was pleased with herself and, more to the point, Debbie was delighted.

"You've done so well, Sally," she told her. "And under very upsetting circumstances. By the way," she went on, "Mum is back home now and says she's got a surprise for me. You must come over for a meal."

Sally hadn't been out and about much lately. Rob's deceit had knocked her self confidence, and she wasn't sure if she wanted to see Sandra, because it might trigger memories of Toby.

Toby, whose hand she had declined to hold, and whose kiss she had refused to think about because she was promised to Rob, yet Rob had had no such compunction.

As she thought of Rob she aimlessly rearranged the tall white enamel jugs on the benching, interspersing them with green ones. Rob had been shamefaced and full of remorse, but the outcome was the same.

"I knew I couldn't live without her," he had explained simply.

"Who is she?" Sally had asked despairingly.

"It's Lili," Rob said, as if it was obvious. "My physiotherapist."

Sally shrugged now, pulling herself together.

"It's over and done with. Water under the bridge."

She glanced down at the aquamarine ring as she rearranged the vases, because that reminded her of the bridge in Annecy and the kiss.

"You are being sentimental and foolish," she admonished herself out loud. "You have built it up into something that it wasn't. It was two people enjoying company in new surroundings."

Mentally giving herself a shake, she locked up the shop and crossed the road to St Andrew's Church to do some measuring, because she had to decorate it for a wedding shortly after the delivery of the first stock of flowers.

Sally loved St Andrew's. She had decorated it numerous times and it always left her feeling peaceful yet invigorated. An odd combination, she thought as she lifted the heavy old latch.

The church wasn't empty. There was a figure at the end of the nave. A clerical figure, yet not the vicar whom she knew quite well.

She clutched the back pew as her head started to spin in an alarming way, because for a second she thought it was Toby. At the sound of her slight gasp, the figure turned.

Toby looked tall and handsome in a grey suit and dog collar, while she was still wearing her green overall, carrying a garden kneeler and iPad.

"Toby?" she faltered.

"Sally!" he cried. "How wonderful it is to see you!"

Swiftly he covered the space between them, although as soon as they were face to face neither seemed to know what to say or do next. But it didn't matter, because the door latch lifted and two more people came into the church chatting cheerfully in French.

Still clutching the pew, Sally felt it must all be a dream as she turned to see Sandra and Albert.

"We didn't expect to see you here, Sally," Sandra said as she kissed her. "It was going to be a surprise for you when you came to Debbie's. We had better explain," she went on.

The explanation was simple, although Sally found it difficult to take it all in, especially as she could feel Toby's eyes on her the whole time.

Sandra was not Sandra Lodge any longer. She was now Madame Joubert after a quiet wedding in France.

"We didn't want any fuss," she explained in her sensible way, and Albert, nodding vigorously, caught Sandra's hand and kissed it flamboyantly.

Sandra and Albert? Married? Sally turned to Toby in bewilderment.

"It's a lot to take in, isn't it?" His smile was just as she remembered it and sent her heart racing. "I'm here because Sandra and Albert wanted a blessing in an English church, and thought of me."

"It took time to track you down, Toby," Sandra interrupted laughingly. "But you were there when Albert and I first met, so we felt it would be fitting."

"We're here to meet the vicar," Toby explained. "To see if it can be arranged."

The door latch clattered yet again and Debbie and the vicar hurried in.

As the group moved up the aisle, Toby caught Sally's arm urgently and swung her round to face him.

"I had to come for Sandra's sake," he whispered, " even though I knew seeing you would be painful."

"Painful?" Sally didn't understand.

Toby picked up her left hand and stared at it. Ringless. No wedding ring. No engagement ring.

His eyes brightened with relief as they met hers.

"Nothing?" he questioned.

"Nothing." Sally's confidence was returning rapidly in the exhilarating tug of attraction that she could feel was still there.

She held up her other hand, where the aquamarine ring caught a ray of sunlight streaming down from a window high up in the nave.

The others were chatting noisily, which made the silence between Sally and Toby seem all the more significant.

"Then we have another chance?" Toby's voice was eager. "Can we continue where we left off all those months ago?"

He gently lifted her trembling hand to his lips, just as he had done at their farewell in Annecy.

"Yes, please," she murmured.

They stood looking into each other's eyes, oblivious of the rest of the party, who had now stopped talking and had turned to look at them.

"I think you may have another wedding in the offing, vicar," Sandra declared in her brisk, carrying voice. "And a jolly good thing, too!" ▪

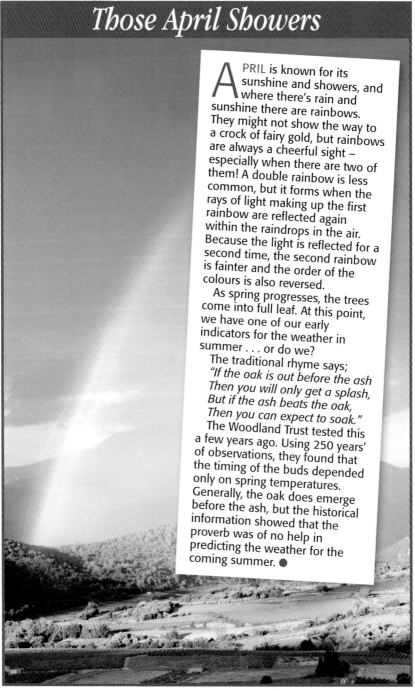

Those April Showers

APRIL is known for its sunshine and showers, and where there's rain and sunshine there are rainbows. They might not show the way to a crock of fairy gold, but rainbows are always a cheerful sight – especially when there are two of them! A double rainbow is less common, but it forms when the rays of light making up the first rainbow are reflected again within the raindrops in the air. Because the light is reflected for a second time, the second rainbow is fainter and the order of the colours is also reversed.

As spring progresses, the trees come into full leaf. At this point, we have one of our early indicators for the weather in summer . . . or do we?

The traditional rhyme says;
*"If the oak is out before the ash
Then you will only get a splash,
But if the ash beats the oak,
Then you can expect to soak."*

The Woodland Trust tested this a few years ago. Using 250 years' of observations, they found that the timing of the buds depended only on spring temperatures. Generally, the oak does emerge before the ash, but the historical information showed that the proverb was of no help in predicting the weather for the coming summer. ●

Strictly For The Birds

by Alice Conway.

MAISIE had never felt cheated because she hadn't married. She had many friends, men and women, and although she hadn't had her own children, her rewarding career as a very successful teacher had been full of children. Some of them were still in her life as friends.

There were other young folk she had met in various ways. One of her favourites was teenager Jamie, whom she got to know when he and his parents had lived next door to her.

He had said he would call by today, and there he was, coming down the road with his dog beside him. Both of them seemed oblivious to the falling rain.

She opened the door that faced the street.

"You should have brought an umbrella!"

Jamie and his little dog ran the last few yards and dripped their way into Maisie's hallway. Jamie slid a surprisingly large pack off his back and put it on the floor.

"Wait there. I'll get some towels." Maisie disappeared and reappeared in seconds. She tossed one towel to Jamie. "Use that one to mop up, then put it under that pack to catch the drips. I'll see to Mickey."

The little terrier heard his name and gave a responsive yap. Maisie bent over to rub his wiry coat.

"Sorry to be a nuisance," Jamie apologised.

"Nuisance? Nonsense. I'm pleased you made the time to come by before your big shift south tomorrow."

Maisie smiled, mainly because she loved the feeling of Mickey's warm body as she towelled him. She did wish, now her life was less busy, that she had a pet. She and Jamie had sometimes discussed it. Jamie, like most teenagers, loved company. He found it difficult to understand how Maisie could be content with life on her own.

"You should get an animal for company. You'd love it. A little dog like Mickey would be good."

"A dog has to be properly looked after," Maisie had told him. "It needs

exercise and I can't guarantee I could walk it every day." She indicated the walking stick in the corner. "I'm far from helpless, but there are days when I depend on that to help me get around. At times I'd be too slow for a bouncing little dog."

"A cat, then. You could get a cat."

"No." Maisie had said this more than once. "A cat would frighten the birds in my garden. I do enjoy seeing them there. They're very entertaining. And you'd be surprised at how many different species come into my back garden."

Maisie turned to Jamie now as he finished drying off.

"I thought you might be held up with jobs to finish at home. I'm going to miss your visits." The little dog trotted across the room and stopped by Maisie's well-used armchair.

"He's waiting for you to sit down so he can jump up on your knee," Jamie told her.

"He'll have to wait until I get our tea out." Maisie headed for the kitchen and her voice floated out over the rattle of teacups and the whistling of the kettle.

"Are you all ready for university?"

"Yep," Jamie called back. "All packed. Wish I could take Mickey."

"Your mum will be glad to look after him. The house will feel empty when you're gone."

Maisie came back into the lounge bearing a tray with a large chocolate cake, two cups and a teapot.

James leaped up to take it.

"Gran Maisie, sit down. I'll pour the tea and cut the cake."

Maisie let him take the tray to the table and she settled into her chair. Mickey jumped on to her lap.

"Gran Maisie," she mused. "You used to call me that all the time when you and your mum lived over the fence."

"I know." Jamie grinned. "I used to think you really were my grandma, not just our neighbour."

Maisie took the cup of tea Jamie offered and put it on the small side table. She wagged a finger at Mickey.

"You sit still now." She turned back to Jamie. "You were the nearest thing to a grandson I was ever going to have. You were a great joy to me, Jamie. I'm going to miss you. Have you got the accommodation arrangements settled?"

"I have." Jamie launched into an explanation relating to the confusion that had ensued over applying for more than one residential hall. Maisie listened to his rapid chatter and watched, with pleasure, how he could still manage to make a very large slice of cake disappear.

WHAT a wonderful thing it had been to watch Jamie grow from a baby to a child and then a teenager. He was heading towards manhood now, but he still hadn't forsaken the enthusiasm and excitement that always been part of his personality. Maisie hoped that it would always stay with him.

"I had to make sure I called today," Jamie added after telling her his parents were going to be driving him down to his new home in the city tomorrow. "There will be no time in the morning. Are there any jobs you need me to do?"

"That's good of you to ask." Maisie smiled. "But there's nothing I need done. Why don't you have some more tea?"

"No, thanks. I've been thinking I might try and get more used to coffee. Lots of people drink coffee these days, especially in the city."

Maisie suppressed a small smile.

"You'll fit in whether you drink tea or coffee, Jamie. No need to worry about that."

Jamie flushed a little.

"I'm not worrying," he protested.

"Of course not," Maisie agreed hastily.

Beside The Sea

THERE'S nothing like a seaside trip
To brighten any day,
The salt sea air dispels all care,
And blows the blues away.
There's nothing like the dancing waves
That swish around your toes;
The water's crash, the diamond splash,
Will wash away all woes.
There's nothing like a good cream tea
To make the world taste sweet.
Or, twice as nice, a strawberry ice
Is just the perfect treat.
There's nothing like your own front door;
How fast the day has sped!
Our trip's been great, but now it's late.
Goodnight, it's time for bed.

– Maggie Ingall.

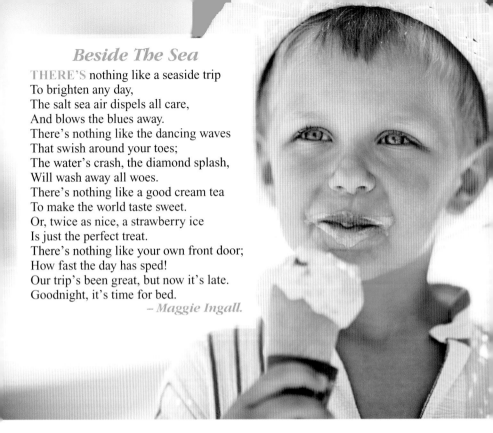

"Gran Maisie, there's one job I would like to do for you," Jamie told her solemnly.

"Is there?"

"Would you stay here with Mickey while I do it? It's a goodbye surprise, you see. It's in the garden. I want to make it ready before you take a look."

"In the garden?" Maisie frowned. "A goodbye surprise?"

"It's stopped raining so I'll dash out now." Jamie stood up.

"Yes, of course. A garden surprise! I can't imagine what it might be."

Before she had finished her last remark, Jamie was out in the hallway and she heard him moving the bulky pack he had arrived with.

"Stay there, Gran Maisie!" he called.

Whatever was he up to, Maisie wondered. What had he brought in that pack? Was it a new plant? She felt slightly nervous if it was. How would he know where to plant it without disturbing some of her other treasured plants?

Mickey turned suddenly in her lap and whined.

"He'll be back," Maisie told him. "Then we'll go outside and see what he's been up to."

She tickled the little dog behind his ears.

71

"I'm glad that you're still going to get to call in and see me," she told him.

Jamie's voice called suddenly from the hallway.

"Come outside now and see what you think!"

MICKEY was down on the floor in a flash and out into the passageway. She heard his little feet patter on the kitchen vinyl as she got up to follow him out to the back garden.

Jamie was standing by the door.

"I know that you'd like a pet, but not a cat or a dog –"

"I'd love either one of those," Maisie protested. "But they don't suit –"

"I know," Jamie interrupted. "But I think this will."

Goodness me, Maisie thought. Surely he hadn't got her some other sort of animal!

She stood on the pathway that curved across her small lawn. The lawn was bordered by gardens bright with annuals and backed by the shrubs and the two trees that the birds so enjoyed. Maisie, to her relief, saw no animal in sight.

Jamie noted her eyes searching in bewilderment.

"Look over here," he said, pointing to one of the trees. "Look what I made for you."

He stepped forward and put a hand lightly on one of the two thin squares of timber threaded one above the other on a chain. The chain was hooked on a tree branch, suspending the two shapes.

"You said you loved the birds in the garden, and I think this will bring even more if you put food out on it every day. It's a bird table."

"Jamie!" Maisie's voice was full of delight. "A two-storey bird table!"

"It's not as good as a dog, I know, but it's kind of like having pets of your own. Birds."

"Jamie, it's wonderful! I shall so enjoy it!"

Jamie's face glowed.

"I hope you will."

Maisie turned back to the kitchen door, beckoning behind her with one hand.

"Let's get some food to put on it right now! I'll find a container."

Jamie followed her in, his face lit brightly because he knew that his gift had been appreciated.

"You won't see me much in future; just when I'm back in the holidays. But you won't forget me, will you? Not with that hanging out there all the time."

Maisie pulled Jamie into a hug.

"Jamie, I wouldn't forget you even if that wonderful goodbye surprise wasn't hanging there! And as soon as we've put some food out for the birds, I'll put the rest of that cake in a box so you can take it home to share with the rest of your family."

"Good plan, Gran Maisie." Jamie grinned. "Good plan." ∎

Clackmannan, Clackmannanshire

THIS unusually named little town in central Scotland owes its origins to the "Clack" or Stone of Mannan, an ancient whinstone boulder named after the Celtic god Manau.

The heart of Clackmannan revolves around its market place at the top of Main Street. Here you will find what remains of the town's Tolbooth. Built at the height of Clackmannan's powers in 1592 as a court, prison and administrative centre, it is only the belfry tower that now survives. Next to it is the Mercat Cross, where markets have been held for centuries. If you look closely, you can still see the marks left by the chains of prisoners whose penalty was to be attached to it.

Another unusual thing about Clackmannan is its harbour. The town's early growth owed much to its port on the River Black Devon, which flowed into the River Forth. Nowadays, however, nothing remains of the port as it was silted up, and the town stands on rising ground at least a mile from the River Forth. ■

Soapbox Summer

by Keith Havers.

H AVEN'T those lads got anything better to occupy themselves with?" Alf rose from his chair to turn the volume up on the TV. "It sounds like World War Three has broken out upstairs."

Bella sighed. She wished Alf wouldn't just slump in front of the box after tea. Once he was settled, there was no shifting him. It wasn't as if he was tired after a hard day's work. If the cricket team were a man short he would be down at the ground in a flash. If there was a darts match on he would be down the pub as soon as they opened.

"They're just letting off steam," she said.

"It's the school holidays. Haven't they had all day to do that?"

"They're just normal, energetic kids. You'd complain if they just moped around the house."

"Can't they go down the park?"

"I don't like letting them go off too far on their own in the evening. They have two main roads to cross. Why don't you take them down there for an hour?"

"Kevin's nine and Luke is nearly eleven. They're old enough to look after themselves."

Bella gave up. Alf was obviously not moving tonight. "Whicker's World" would be on later, which was one of his favourites. It was just a good job "Z Cars" or "The Saint" wasn't on tonight or he would really be annoyed with the kids.

Thankfully they would be in bed by the time the news came on. Alf was eager to hear of any developments on what the papers were calling the Great Train Robbery.

"They'll never catch those guys," he had said when the news first broke. "There's obviously a criminal mastermind behind that. Too clever for our cops."

Bella was too busy keeping the peace in her own home without bothering about fugitives from the law.

Illustration by André Leonard.

"I'll tell you what," Alf said. "If you can keep them quiet tonight, I'll spend the whole weekend with them."

"All weekend? Are you sure?"

"You're right," Alf admitted. "I remember me and their uncle Pete driving our dad out of his mind when we were kids. I'll find something to keep them occupied."

Bella had her doubts, but Alf was as good as his word. As soon as the boys were up and fed on Saturday morning he walked them down to the recreation ground with a football and a bottle of squash.

Bella had just finished cleaning the oven and wiping down the kitchen shelves when they got home.

"I suppose you want some lunch now," she said.

"Dad bought us chips," Kevin said.

"And mushy peas," Luke added.

"I bought you a piece of cod," Alf told her. "You should have it now while it's hot."

After her busy morning Bella was pleasantly surprised that Alf was being so helpful. He had always been a great dad, but sometimes she thought he treated the boys as young adults rather than children. Even Luke, the elder, needed a little playtime with his dad.

"I'm glad I got the jobs done this morning," she said. "I suppose you'll be watching cricket on the TV this afternoon."

"The boys have asked if they can go for a bike ride tomorrow. I thought I'd get my old boneshaker out of the shed and give it an oiling."

"That bike hasn't seen the light of day for over a year," Bella said. "It'll probably need more than an oiling."

Nevertheless, Alf took the two boys outside to get their machines ready for the next day while Bella finished her lunch. With the boys from under her feet she took the opportunity to go upstairs and tidy their room.

Apart from toys and games there seemed to be a mountain of comics spilling over in the corner. Luke never wanted to throw any of them away. Bella didn't mind the "Beano" or the "Dandy" comics, but just lately he had been getting a few of the American ones from other boys at school. She wasn't sure if he was old enough for action heroes like Batman and Superman. Having said that, Dennis the Menace wasn't exactly the perfect role model!

I WONDER how they're getting on?"

Nearly two hours had gone by while Bella put away the toys and sorted out the comics.

"It shouldn't take this long to clean up their bikes. Maybe I was right and Alf's just isn't roadworthy. The lads will be really disappointed if he can't take them out now that he's promised."

She made her way to the back of the garden, to find Alf and the two boys amongst a pile of junk.

"What on earth is going on?"

"Hello, love," Alf said. "We got a bit diverted."

"What happened to getting the bikes ready?"

"The kids' bikes are OK. But mine was jammed against the back wall. We've had to take all this stuff out to get at it."

Bella looked around at the rubbish that littered the back yard. A rusty lawnmower, a battered pram and a broken pushchair lay amongst a collection of other bits and pieces. Various unidentifiable machine parts, planks of wood and lengths of piping barred her from approaching any closer.

"I hadn't realised I'd let the place get into such a state," Alf admitted.

"You might as well leave it out here for the rag-and-bone man to collect next week," Bella said.

"Oh, no, Dad!" Luke cried. "Can we have the pram wheels to make a box-cart?"

"Yeah," Kevin agreed. "Just like the Bash Street Kids in the 'Beano'."

"You've both got bicycles," Bella argued. "Why do you need a cart?"

"We could build two and have races," Luke explained.

"Yeah!" Kevin shouted.

"Don't get so excited, you two," Bella said. "I don't want you messing around with any of this stuff. It's filthy and dangerous."

"Oh, Mum!" they wailed in unison.

"It wouldn't hurt to let them try to make something," Alf soothed. "I'll keep my eye on them and it'll keep them occupied."

"Can we, Mum?"

"Oh, and you were right about my old bike," he said.

Bella spotted a dilapidated heap propped against the garden fence.

"The chain has rusted solid and the tyres are perished."

Bella sighed. She had no argument against the idea. The boys had something to keep them busy and out of mischief, and Alf seemed willing to spend time with them.

"All right, but be careful."

She returned to the house with mixed feelings. This wasn't the sort of activity she had had in mind for the boys. Pleased that her husband seemed to be enjoying himself as much as the kids, she still wasn't sure if messing around with scrap metal and wood offcuts was a suitable way to fill their time.

"I suppose I should be careful what I wish for," she told herself.

FOR the rest of the afternoon Bella left them to it. She heard hammering and sawing and a few shouts and squeals. Her heart leaped as she imagined the pair with sharp edges and wood splinters. Thankfully the howls were of delight and they all came in ravenous at teatime.

"I hope you're watching them closely," Bella said. "I don't want to be patching them up with sticking plasters and antiseptic cream."

"They're having the time of their lives," Alf told her. "You should be pleased that they're channelling their energy into something creative."

Right now Bella was pleased that Alf was channelling his efforts into bonding with his children. He appeared to have found the ideal way to keep them amused.

"Well, go and clean yourselves up. You're not sitting down at the table with dirty hands."

Before bedtime Alf had helped his sons construct two decent carts. With the fading light, it was extremely difficult to persuade the boys that there was no time to test them out, other than a short push up and down the garden path.

B Y the time Alf got home from the factory the next day his boys were desperate to try out their vehicles. Bella hadn't had the time nor the confidence to take them out herself.

"Dad, Dad!" the boys chorused. "Can we take the carts up to the rec?"

He had to wolf his tea down and get changed while his sons fidgeted on the sofa in anticipation.

"Why don't you come with us, love?" he asked Bella. "The washing-up can wait."

"Yeah, Mum! Come and watch us race down the hill."

Bella wasn't sure she wanted to see her kids hurtling down a steep slope, but it was a pleasant evening and her presence might curb their wilder instincts. Alf led the way while, behind him, the boys pulled their carts with Bella bringing up the rear.

Luke's cart had two small pushchair wheels at the front and two larger ones from a bicycle at the back. A soap crate provided the seating and a length of rope provided something to steer by. Kevin's used four pram wheels with just a plywood board to sit on.

Bella was somewhat disturbed to note that neither cart had brakes.

A grass bank at the far end of the park sloped gently upwards at first before rising steeply and finishing on a plateau. As they made their way towards it a few of the boys' schoolfriends happened along and were eager to observe the proceedings.

"I think you should start just halfway up," Bella suggested. "Take it carefully to begin with."

A small crowd had gathered now to see the maiden launch of the two carts. Bella was a little apprehensive as her elder son propelled himself down the slight gradient with one kick of his heel. To her relief he rolled along the rough grass with barely a wobble and came to rest at the foot of the slope. Kevin followed suit and the two boys trudged back up together, hauling their carriages behind them.

"We want to start from the top!" Luke and Kevin called before they had got halfway back.

Bella looked at Alf for reassurance.

"They'll be fine," he said.

Bella noticed that the crowd appeared to have swelled even more and that the escapades of her two young boys were generating a great deal of excitement. Time after time, as they trundled down the slope side by side, she heard murmurs of admiration and envy.

My Little Red Suitcase

I'M packing my little red suitcase
For a holiday down by the sea,
But the weather folk just changed the forecast
And it's seriously bothering me!

I'd put in my sun hat and sun cream,
My swimsuit and beach towel, too.
Now they're promising gales and bucketing rain
So my previous list is taboo!

In go the brolly and waterproofs,
My sensible shoes and my socks.
My chunkiest jumper, my scarf and my gloves
Alongside my shorts and my frocks.

Yes, I'm hedging my bets for each season
Ready for all, come what may.
For, although it's supposed to be summertime here,
We can see the whole lot in one day!

I zip up my suitcase in triumph;
I've mastered the challenge, I guess.
But I think that next year I'll "vacation" at home
And simply avoid all the stress!
— *Marian Cleworth.*

iStock.

Eventually her boys tired of dragging their new toys up the hill and were easily persuaded to save their energy for another day. As they retraced their way home Alf and the boys had to field various questions about how they built these machines and where they found the materials.

"I'm really proud of you," Bella said to Alf after the boys had been put to bed. "I've never seen the boys so stimulated."

"I've enjoyed it, too," Alf admitted. "They're good lads really."

"Of course they are," Bella said. "They're our lads."

Arriving home from work the next day, Alf expected a repeat of the night before, but what greeted him defied all expectations. He had walked barely half the distance from the bus stop to his front door when he was accosted

79

by half a dozen of the boys who had been playing in the park the night before.

Kevin and Luke came skipping along the footpath as he turned the street corner.

"Dad! Dad! All our friends want to build carts so we can run our own Soapbox Derby."

"Good grief!" Alf said. "Give me a chance to get through the front door."

He managed to thread his way through the mêlée and sat down at the kitchen table.

"Their friends have been round our back garden all day," Bella said. "I had to shoo them away at dinnertime and I've been giving them orange squash and jam sandwiches all afternoon."

After having his tea and spending a few minutes glancing through the newspaper, Alf got up and peered through the back window. Kevin, Luke and a few of their friends were taking turns to sit in the carts to be pushed a few feet along the garden path.

"They've been doing that all day," Bella said. "Some of them brought planks of wood along and a couple of old tricycles, but I sent them home. We've enough junk in our own yard without adding to it."

"I was hoping for a quiet night," Alf said. "I didn't expect all this fuss. What have I started?"

Bella smiled. All she wanted Alf to do a few days ago was spend an hour or two with his sons. Now he had half the kids in the street knocking at the door and asking for his help!

"Why don't you get together with the other dads?" she suggested. "They ought to get involved with their own kids."

Alf's facial expression told Bella that he had his doubts. Since they had lived here Alf had been the bloke to whom everyone came for any practical help.

When the fellow next door had problems with his motorbike it was Alf who fixed it for him. A few days after the young couple across the street had moved in, Alf was showing the chap how to hang wallpaper. Most of the others had called on Alf for one reason or another. Bella knew that her idea had its drawbacks.

"I'll go and tell those lads to fetch their dads round here," he said.

Within half an hour a little group had gathered in Alf and Bella's back yard. Alf spent several minutes explaining how to remove wheels from prams and bicycles and the best way to attach them to wooden crates.

"I have a few saws and a couple of hammers if anyone needs tools," he said.

Bella watched from the back window as he distributed screws and nails to his neighbours. Seeing him take charge and instruct the other blokes in carpentry and metalwork caused a surge of pride to run through her. Alf was a dad in a million.

T HE following weekend saw a dozen carts racing down the grass slope. It was a holiday atmosphere, with mums and dads all cheering on their offspring.

"It was a good idea of yours to bring some tools along," Alf said to his wife. "I've already been called upon for a few running repairs."

"I have the ideas, you have the skills." Bella laughed.

She was delighted to see everybody enjoying the camaraderie. She gave Luke a shilling to get himself and his brother an ice-cream.

"It's been a marvellous summer," she said as she watched her two boys race off towards the kiosk.

"It surely has," Alf agreed. "They'll be back to school soon, though."

It had certainly been an eventful summer on the global newsfront, with several train robbers already under arrest and Dr Martin Luther King having his famous dream.

But Alf was no longer such an avid follower of world events. By the time the summer holiday drew to a close there had been a couple more get-togethers like this one, and some of the dads had suggested forming some sort of youth club to keep the kids occupied during the winter evenings.

"It looks like you won't be watching as much TV as before," Bella said one night after they had put the kids to bed.

"I don't mind," Alf said. "Time with my family is more precious than watching some globe-trotting journalist on the telly."

"Or worrying about the Royal Mail train being hijacked?"

"There will always be time to keep up with the news," Alf replied.

"And I'm sure you will always be willing to give your opinion on it."

Bella refrained from reminding him of his prediction about the incompetent police squad never catching any of the gang.

"It looks like you're going to be busy for one or two nights a week."

"I don't mind that, either. It's been a lot of fun for me as well as the boys. The blokes round here are all right. We get on well together."

Bella hadn't felt so content for a long time. Her man had grown closer to his sons, the boys had a new-found respect for their dad and the neighbourhood had become more hospitable. She wondered if any of these things would have happened if Alf's bike had been roadworthy and they had gone on that bike ride, after all.

"Strange how things turn out."

"What's that, love?"

"Nothing." She smiled. "Come on. Let's have a quiet night for a change and snuggle up in front of the TV." ∎

Stormy Weather

A WAG once described an English summer as "three hot days and a thunderstorm." No wonder, then, that we make use of every helpful sign to let us know whether or not we might need a brolly when we venture out. One of the most trusted proverbs is:

Red sky at night, shepherd's delight,
Red sky in the morning, shepherd's warning.

It comes from St Matthew's Gospel, in slightly different words, so it has stood the test of time and is one of the more trusted sayings, although it's the red sky around the sun and not the colour of the clouds that counts here.

If we are lucky enough to have a spell of good weather, the pollen in the air can cause hay fever for some people – and for some cats and dogs! A good old thunderstorm usually clears the air, though. The flash of lightning through the air, and the noise created by the rapid heating and expansion of the air around it, make for some spectacular sound and light shows in the summer months.

It's not true that lightning can't strike twice in the same place. The Empire State Building in New York receives around 100 hits per year, and the late Roy C. Sullivan, a former park ranger, had the dubious honour of having survived seven lightning strikes in the course of his life. ●

Illustration by Mandy Dixon/iStock.

Acting The Part

by Susan Blackburn.

ESPITE every effort the tears came. Alone in her rubbish tip of a back garden, Pippa collapsed to her knees on the scratchy patch of green that tried valiantly to pass for a lawn.

Once the storm had subsided, Pippa became aware of another presence. Lifting her head slightly, her eyes alighted on a pair of smart sandals.

"Are you all right, my dear?" a melodious voice enquired, then tutted. "Silly question, you're obviously not all right. I'm Felicity Reynolds; I live next door. I just called round to welcome you to the neighbourhood." She paused then continued in wry tones. "It would appear the neighbourhood has been unsuccessful in making you welcome so far."

Scrambling to her feet, Pippa took in the rest of her visitor. Alert eyes sparkled from a smiling middle-aged face, beautiful and full of character.

"I'm sorry to intrude," Felicity said. "I'll go."

"No, please don't." Pippa shrivelled at the thought of being alone again. "Pippa Marriot. If you'll excuse the mess and I can locate the kettle, I'll make us a drink."

Felicity eyed Pippa over her mug of tea.

"Why were you crying, Pippa? Is it anything I can help with?" she enquired so matter of factly it made Pippa, usually ill at ease with strangers, relax.

It all came out. Her husband Lenny's redundancy, his inability to find another job, him feeling like a total failure.

"Then he went out one day with his best friend and came home eager to join the Army! Good money and fantastic training, he told me." Pippa ran her fingers through her hair.

"He was so passionate about it." She felt about for a tissue as the tears started again. "Although I was terrified at the thought of where he could end up, I couldn't do anything but agree, could I? It was a job and Lenny desperately needed one. So I hid my feelings and put on a brave face. But, in the meantime, we'd already got the move here arranged. Lenny thought moving to a large city would give us more chance of employment."

Pippa wiped her eyes again.

"We got this house for a song as it needs so much done to it, but it was something we were going to do once we'd both found other jobs. By the time everything was sorted with him, all the dates clashed. I've had to organise it all myself." She blew her nose hard. "Goodness, don't I sound like a whinger? I'm usually a lot more positive than this."

Then she gave a faint smile.

"I don't think I've ever opened up like that to a stranger before. You're incredibly easy to talk to."

Felicity squeezed her hand.

"It will have done you good to talk, my dear," she said. "I suspect you've been bottling things up for a while."

"I put a brave face on for my parents, too," Pippa admitted. "They were worried enough with Lenny joining up like that, never mind me starting a new life on my own in a strange place."

Pippa picked at the tissue in her hand and gave Felicity a watery smile.

"I'm so sorry you found me like that. I suddenly felt I needed some air. I guess everything just got on top of me." She blew her nose again. "I miss Lenny so much."

"Well, of course you do, my dear." Felicity patted her hand.

"There are so many trouble spots he could be sent to. It's such a worry."

"It is," Felicity said. "It's always hard on the wives."

Pippa stared at her.

"Both my husband and son were in the Forces, Pippa," Felicity explained. "They came through fine, but my husband hadn't been home very long before

I lost him. He was quite a bit older than me. My son met an American girl and he lives there now, so I don't get to see them, or my grandchildren, very often. We Skype each other, of course, but it's not the same. Especially when all I long to do is hug them all."

Clearing her throat, Felicity stood up.

"But I count my blessings," she said. "I have wonderful friends and a full life. Well, my dear, I must go. It's lovely to have met you. Pop your phone number down for me, and I'll be in touch."

PIPPA tried to "count her blessings" after her neighbour had gone, but failed dismally. All she could see was life in a strange town where she knew nobody except Felicity who, for all her kindness, would probably not bother with her now she'd been such a misery. Her family was miles away and her husband was at the other side of the world.

Unearthing sheets and a duvet, she trudged upstairs to make up her bed. Perhaps she'd feel better after a good night's sleep.

She quickly fell into a dreamless sleep and awoke to the sound of her phone ringing.

"Pippa? It's Felicity. How are you this lovely Saturday morning?"

"Loads better, thank you."

To her surprise, Pippa found it was true. She did feel more positive this morning. Maybe because the sun was streaming into her bedroom.

"Well, I've a few people coming for coffee this morning, and if you'd like to join us you would be more than welcome."

Pippa's heart sank. A roomful of strangers was her worst nightmare. Her natural shyness always meant it took her ages to make friends.

"It's very kind of you, Felicity," she found herself saying, "but really, I've so much to do. Thank you for thinking of me."

Hanging up, Pippa felt the tears start again. How could she make a new life for herself like this?

A few minutes later the doorbell rang. Shrugging on her dressing-gown, wondering who on earth it could be, Pippa ran down the stairs.

"I would have thought it was more important to meet your new neighbours than do jobs all by yourself," her new neighbour said mildly. "If you really want to be alone then say so and I'll go away."

"Come in." Pippa waved Felicity into the kitchen and reached for the kettle. "I'm not very good with new people," she admitted.

"You seem perfectly at ease with me," Felicity said.

"Well, we sort of got thrown in the deep end," Pippa said, then chortled despite herself. "I did just about drown us in my tears."

"True," Felicity acknowledged with a grin. "Anyway, trust me. They're a lovely crowd. We all go to the local leisure club, do various classes there. And they're all very curious, in the nicest possible way, to meet my new neighbour."

"I don't think I can." Pippa could feel the familiar fear welling up in her at the thought.

"I used to be very shy," Felicity began. "Then, because of the high rank to which Frank rose in the Air Force, we had to do quite a lot of entertaining. I had no choice but to get over it. To help me, I used what I called the Stage of Life."

"What's that?"

"I pretended I was acting a part. My cue was the arrival of a guest, and I had to play my part. Don't get me wrong, it was the hardest thing I've ever done, and it obviously wouldn't work for everyone. But it worked for me." She gave Pippa's hand a squeeze. "Give it a go, my dear. After all, what have you got to lose?"

What had she to lose? She could always come home again. Pippa drew a deep breath.

"OK."

"Good. Come over about half ten and I'll show you around. The others won't be arriving until around eleven o'clock and I promise I'll introduce you one by one."

FELICITY'S home was furnished with exquisite taste.

"It's gorgeous, Felicity!" Pippa breathed. "I know who to come to for advice on doing up our house, at least."

"Thank you. It would be a pleasure," Felicity said.

At that moment the doorbell rang. Pippa's heart started to thud.

"Now, Pippa, stand by the fireplace and take deep breaths. When I introduce you your lines are something like, 'Hello, it's great to meet you.' Back in a moment."

Felicity ushered in the first arrival. A round vision in scarlet bounced into the room.

"Hi, you must be Pippa! How lovely to meet you. I'm Lorraine."

"Hello. Great to meet you, too." Pippa also managed a smile along with her words, despite her pounding heart.

"Nothing wrong with that performance," Felicity whispered as she handed Pippa her coffee.

A tall, angular lady, who looked on the fierce side until she smiled, turned out to be Angela. Chloe was a tiny person, with a gorgeous raspy voice. Pippa was in turn introduced to Pauline, Sue, Diane, Judy and Maureen, and was welcomed with such genuine kindness that her anxiety soon faded away. By the time they'd had coffee, Pippa, much to her amazement, felt almost one of the crowd.

As they said goodbye they all told her she should come along to the classes at the leisure club.

Well, perhaps she could, Pippa thought, her spirits rising slightly.

"Would you like to come to the local WI meeting with me, Pippa?" Felicity asked over coffee on a beautiful summer's day a few weeks later.

They were sitting in Pippa's garden on a rather larger patch of green, which could definitely be described as a lawn. Pippa had worked hard to transform the garden, which was now a riot of colour. Felicity had been as good as her word and Pippa was thrilled with the décor and soft furnishings of her new home.

At least with what they had put by, and with Lenny now earning good money, she had been able to enjoy concentrating on the house and garden, before she looked around for another job.

Now Pippa nearly dropped one of her gorgeous new china mugs.

"Pardon me? Did you say the WI?"

Felicity chuckled.

"Despite all you've assumed about the WI, our branch is more 'Calendar Girls' than 'Jam And Jerusalem', I can tell you," she said. "In fact, most branches are. And we have all age groups." She fished in her bag, pulling out a card. "The speaker this time is Julia Monroe who used to work as a make-up artist for the BBC. Should be interesting."

It was! A compelling speaker, Julia regaled them with hilarious anecdotes and happenings behind the scenes at the BBC.

YOU know, Felicity, I can never thank you enough," It was the day before Christmas Eve and Pippa gave her dearest friend a hug. "You gave me confidence just when I needed it most, and who would have thought I'd have the courage to do this? Lenny home for Christmas and in the audience is just the icing on the cake. Oh, my!" she breathed, clutching Felicity in terror. "I'm so nervous. What if I forget what I'm doing?"

"Natural fears, my dear. We all have them before we go on. Now, deep breaths. Lenny will be so proud of you, and so am I," Felicity said, giving Pippa a hug. "Knock 'em dead!"

Attired in her maid's uniform, Pippa waited, heart thumping, in the wings for her cue, then strode on to the stage clutching a laden tray.

"Your afternoon tea, madam," she said in ringing tones, placing the tray carefully on the table. "Will there be anything else?"

"No, thank you, Carter, that will be all."

Pippa exited stage left, heart singing.

One line in a WI play. But to Pippa another massive step forward on the Stage of Life. ▌

Illustration by Ruth Blair.

A Stitch In Time

by Catriona McCuaig.

SARAH MOORE and Jim Paterson had been best friends for ever. That is, until Sheila Gleason came on the scene, when everything changed in the blink of an eye.

From the moment Sheila walked into the bank on her first day, Jim had been head over heels in love, with no time left over for Sarah or anyone else.

"Don't you mind?" Sarah's friend Jenny wanted to know, having watched the budding romance unfold from day to day.

"Of course I don't mind," Sarah assured her. "Jim had to get married sooner or later, and if Sheila is what he wants, then I'm happy for him."

Sarah could tell from the frown on her friend's face that she didn't believe a word of it. Come to that, Sarah wasn't sure she believed it herself!

She had first set eyes on Jim when she was a six-year-old at the village school.

"This is Jim," Miss Roberts announced. "Say hello to Jim, everybody!"

"Hello, Jim!" the children cried in singsong voices.

Suddenly shy, Jim hung his head. He was a wiry, tow-headed boy, wearing neat jeans and a bright red shirt.

"Jim's family has just moved to Bingham so he doesn't know anyone here," Miss Roberts went on. "I'm sure you'll all make him feel welcome."

It was a foregone conclusion that the newcomer would be paired with Sarah. She was sitting alone in the old-fashioned two-person desk, and every other seat was already taken. Red-faced, Jim took up his place to the accompaniment of unkind laughter from the other boys.

Sarah was too embarrassed to look at him. Oh, the shame of having to sit with a boy! Her friends were sure to tease her when they went outside at playtime.

It was even worse when it was time to go home and she found herself walking in the same direction as the newcomer. It turned out that Jim's family had moved into a house just two doors away from Sarah.

Fortunately the problem soon righted itself. Their parents became friends, and before long Sarah and Jim were best pals, spending every waking moment together.

The years passed, but nothing changed between them. Sarah could often be seen jumping up and down at the edge of the football field, cheering Jim on, and she never had to worry about finding a boy to take her to the school dance, because Jim was ready and willing to escort her.

When the world of work beckoned, both chose a career in banking, after which their mothers confidently predicted a future which involved at least two shared grandchildren.

Then came Sheila. It was only natural that she wanted Jim all to herself without Sarah playing gooseberry. But did she have to frown quite so grimly when she found Jim and Sarah exchanging a joke at the copying machine? Or make a catty remark when Jim happened to compliment Sarah on her new blouse?

"I can take a hint," Sarah told Jenny. "I'm going to apply for a transfer."

"You can't let that woman drive you away," Jenny protested.

"It's about time I moved on if I want to get promotion anyway," Sarah argued. "And who knows, Mr Right may be waiting for me just around the corner."

Sarah applied for her transfer and in due course found herself in Hartswell, a town 50 miles away. She found a comfortable little flat on a quiet street, and soon learned her way about the town, yet there seemed to be something missing. Her new colleagues were pleasant enough, but they didn't provide companionship outside the office. The two men were already married, and the women were either married or in established relationships. They had no time to spare for Sarah.

With a shock, she realised she was lonely. It was a new experience for her, for whenever she'd wanted company in the past all she had to do was squeeze through the hedge that separated her childhood home from Jim's. He was always ready to join her in whatever scheme she had in mind.

Something had to be done about it. What was it the agony aunts said in women's magazines? Join a club. Do volunteer work. Take a course. Find a new hobby.

So Sarah visited the library to see what was available.

"How about learning to knit?" the librarian suggested when Sarah had wrinkled her nose at the thought of pot-holing, photography and learning to tap-dance. "It's something you can do anywhere, and this course is worthwhile because everything you make while you're learning is donated to charity."

That sounded good to Sarah. When she was a teenager her gran had offered to teach her to knit, but it hadn't appealed. Now, though, it seemed like a useful craft she could learn while making like-minded friends here in Hartswell at the same time. What could be better?

* * * *

The instructor was a cheerful, white-haired lady called Mrs Meredith.

"Call me Mabel," she told the assembled group. "For the first few sessions you'll be working here until you gain confidence, and after that you can knit as much as you wish in your spare time and bring your projects to the weekly meetings for my inspection. At first we'll make squares that will be sewn together to make blankets for the Red Cross, and later you'll move on to items of your choice. Once you're past the frustration of learning the basics you'll find that knitting is a relaxing and most enjoyable hobby."

Sarah gasped in admiration when Mabel took them to view examples of her own work, displayed on a table. An Aran jacket displaying a variety of intricate cables, honeycombs and trinity stitches; a jumper with a Fair Isle yoke in gorgeous colours; a cot blanket in a lacy pattern.

"I'll never be able to tackle anything like this," she said.

"Don't worry," Mabel said, laughing. "This sort of thing is for my advanced class. Mind you, it's not as hard as it looks. There are basically two stitches in knitting, what we call plain and purl. Everything else is simply a variation on the two. Take this, for instance." She pointed to the ribbing of the pretty mohair jumper she had on. "It's simply knit one, purl one. But it's time to stop talking and get down to business." She turned to the class. "Take your places, everyone, and I'll show you how to cast on."

By the third session Sarah had chosen to make a pair of purple mittens and, after a few false starts, she had managed to complete the ribbing. Why was it that the mistakes didn't show themselves until several rows further on and you had to carefully unpick the lot?

Still, it was fascinating work, and she enjoyed herself when she joined several of the other women for coffee at the Copper Kettle after class.

The mitten progressed well. After doing battle with the thumb, Sarah found herself on the home straight, working steadily in stocking stitch until it was time to start decreasing, which she very much enjoyed.

"Well done!" Mabel said, looking over her shoulder. "Shall I show you how to sew it up?"

A short while later Sarah gazed proudly at the finished product while her new friends clapped and cheered. She felt elated when Mabel suggested that she could start work on the other mitten at home and she readily agreed to go it alone until the next meeting.

"Mittens lend themselves to all sorts of embellishment," Mabel observed. "You can embroider flowers on a plain mitten, or you can knit them in stripes, or work in cables or diamonds. The sky's the limit!"

*　*　*　*

At home the following evening, Sarah worked away happily on the second mitten, looking from time to time at the printed instruction sheet she'd been given. It all went so well that she managed to complete it, overjoyed to think she would actually have a completed pair to show when she arrived at class.

"Very nicely done," Mabel approved. "Where's the other one? Do let us see the pair together."

Sarah rummaged in her bag. She hadn't looked at the first mitten since it had been completed.

Oh, no! Something didn't look right! What on earth could have happened?

"I don't understand," she faltered. "I thought I did everything right, but . . ."

"Let me see." Calmly, Mabel picked up the two mittens, turning them over in her hand. "They are beautifully knitted," she murmured. "It's just that you've made two for the same hand. If you look carefully at your pattern you'll find that instructions for the left hand are given on the back of the page."

"I feel such a fool," Sarah mumbled, feeling her face grow hot.

"You've done remarkably well for a beginner," Mabel said, smiling kindly.

"I can't bear the thought of unpicking it right down to the top of the ribbing."

"Ah, I have a solution to that, my dear. We have plenty of matching wool in stock, so why not make two left-hand mittens next? Then we'll have two excellent pairs which will go to two lucky children, instead of only one."

As one woman in the class broke into applause, Sarah beamed.

"Mabel, you're a genius!" she said.

"Far from it, my dear. Knitting is a metaphor for life. Don't waste time fretting over your mistakes; just learn from them and move on. If you've dropped a stitch, pick it up. If you don't like the pattern you're working on, choose a new one. Wrong colour for your complexion? Try a different one next time."

Mabel's words of homespun wisdom echoed through Sarah's mind as, working diligently, she produced two more mittens. When the phone rang just as she was casting off for the final time, she decided not to pick it up, but it kept ringing and ringing until she was forced to answer it.

"Look, I don't know who you are, but if you're selling something I don't want it!"

"Sarah, it's me! Please listen to what I have to say!"

"Jim? Is that you? What's up? There's nothing wrong at home, is there?" Sarah was worried.

"Your folks are fine. I thought I'd come up and see you this weekend if you're not doing anything important."

Sarah frowned.

"Won't Sheila have something to say about that?"

"I'm not seeing Sheila any more. We don't have anything in common."

"You mean she's the wrong colour for your complexion!" Sarah laughed to herself.

"What on earth are you talking about?"

"Oh, just something someone said."

"So can I come?" Jim repeated.

"I suppose so, since you seem to be at a loose end."

"Oh, Sarah, it's not just that. I've missed you since you've been away. Seeing Sheila was exciting and fun, but all the while I was overlooking something valuable that was right underneath my nose. I love you, Sarah. I'm hoping you feel the same. Is there any chance for me at all?"

A warm glow swept through her, like sunshine coming out after the rain.

"I suppose I could try picking up a dropped stitch or two, given time," she said.

"You're making no sense at all!" he complained. "What's the matter with you?"

"Just come up at the weekend and we'll talk about it then. Can't stop now, Jim. Got to get back to my knitting. See you soon."

She switched off her phone, ignoring his squawks of protest, but she didn't touch her needles and yarn again that evening. She had a lot of thinking to do.

She'd made a silly mistake with those mittens, but with a bit of extra work she'd managed to put it right and something beautiful had resulted. And she realised now that in coming to Hartswell and leaving Jim behind she'd changed a pattern that hadn't needed changing at all.

But now she'd been given a chance to put matters right and she was ready to grasp it with both hands, even if she was wearing two small pairs of beautifully knitted mittens while she did it. Metaphorically speaking, of course! ■

Brighton Pier, Brighton

THE history of Brighton's pier goes back to 1823, when it was called the Old Chain Pier and was used as a landing stage for passenger ships that sailed from Dieppe in France. The owners, however, saw a chance to make money and began charging an entry fee of 2d to allow visitors access to kiosks and entertainment stalls.

The pier was closed in May 1940, as it was seen by the War Office to be potentially useful to seaborne invasion forces. In fact, the War Office instructed that an entire section of the Palace Pier be removed and it was put under guard at all times.

If you feel as if J. Campbell Kerr's illustration of Brighton Pier looks remarkably familiar, you might be remembering it from its starring roles in the following films – "Carry On At Your Convenience" in 1971, "Quadrophenia" in 1979, "The End Of The Affair" in 1999 and "Sweeney Todd: The Demon Barber Of Fleet Street" in 2007. ■

93

The Party Planner

by Em Barnard.

JOYCE, mobile in hand, pen and notebook on the dining table, plus blank invitation cards, looked at her husband across from her. All she wanted was a family party for their golden wedding anniversary. But Les seemed like he couldn't care less about it.

"But we always have our party the closest Sunday to the date," she urged. "It falls *on* a Sunday this year – you can't get closer than that! Les, this is important," she said when he hunched deeper over his gardening book. "Who are we inviting? And we need to book the venue. They soon get full during the summer."

"And I have to get these cuttings done. Leave it till this evening." He closed his manual and made a hasty escape with it to his greenhouse.

Joyce was miffed. She'd had no problem with him as far as booking the two of them into the Haven, a country hotel they often frequented for a weekend, went. She'd booked it for the Friday night in anticipation of the celebration party on the Sunday.

What was his problem? She frowned as she tidied the stack of invitation cards. Could it be that the family had already organised a surprise party for her? Maybe Julie had had a word with her dad to make sure Joyce didn't arrange something.

Joyce had grown up being in charge. She was the eldest and only girl with three younger brothers, and had helped her widowed mother keep them in check. So much so that in her late teens many a boyfriend had backed off, alarmed by a strong-minded female.

But Les was wise and quick-witted and had a way of talking her round. She found she rather liked having someone else making the decisions sometimes, taking the worry of life away. But over their 50 years together, there were still times when her domineering nature came through.

She wandered into the lounge. The doors through to the conservatory were open for the summer warmth to invade. As she entered, she heard Les talking to their daughter on his mobile.

"Julie? Your mum's been at it again. She wants to book this party at

Illustration by Kirk Houston/Thinkstockphotos.

Fountains Hall. I can't keep putting her off. If she phones the place, she might find out you've already booked it for the following Sunday! It's a nuisance they were booked solid for our special day. Any ideas on how to put her off?"

Joyce slipped back into the dining-room. So she was right – it *was* a surprise party! OK, she'd play along. Even though it wasn't on the day of their anniversary, the thought was there, and she'd still have their overnight stay at the Haven to look forward to.

S HE had told the whole family there wasn't anything she wanted in the way of presents; that she just needed everyone she loved around her. That went for Les, too. Nevertheless, he'd booked Joyce in for an afternoon of pampering at the Haven while they were there – massage, make-over, and a hair appointment.

Soon it was the Saturday evening and they were taking a last stroll through the glorious grounds of the hotel down to the glittering river that passed it.

"I hope you've enjoyed our overnight break, Joyce," Les said as they stood at the river's side and watched the ducks sailing on the water.

"You know I have, especially the pampering," she replied, squeezing his arm.

"Then I have a further surprise for you," he told her. "We're staying over another night."

"Really?" She blinked at him.

He pushed back a gold-grey curl from her forehead and folded it in with the others.

"It's because tomorrow – our anniversary – might be a bit of a let-down. You've been really good in not pushing me about booking Fountains Hall. You see, Julie couldn't get tomorrow when she went to book it so . . ." He paused. "It's next Sunday instead."

"Oh, Les, that's fine," Joyce assured him, hoping she sounded surprised. "But you'll have to wait till we get home tomorrow for your present. I didn't expect us to be staying here a second night."

"As long as I have you, I don't need presents," he said, taking her in his arms and pressing his lips against hers. "But as we're on the subject . . ." he began, reaching into his pocket. "I should really save this for tomorrow, but I want to give it to you now. Happy golden wedding anniversary, Joyce."

He presented her with a small, red velvet box. She sprang the lid.

"A diamond eternity ring! Oh, Les, it's beautiful."

He slipped it on her finger and they kissed again, and in an embrace they watched the sun sink behind the trees.

G O and doll yourself up, Joyce."
Joyce, relaxing on a lounger on the sunny patio, opened her eyes to see Les looking down at her. He was dressed in his best cream shirt and grey trousers.

"Another surprise? But we're about to have lunch."

"Are you complaining?"

"No," she said, pulling herself upright.

"Off you go, then. Put that new pink dress on. You haven't worn it yet."

As the car rocked gently through the sun-warmed countryside half an hour later, Joyce smiled over the wonderful weekend she'd had. So Les was still pampering her. Was he thinking of stopping off for lunch somewhere?

Her mind went to the smartphone she'd bought him with the help of Julie. She and Julie had had their own secret, putting him off buying one, saying there was an even newer model coming if he'd hold on a couple of months. She could hear his yelp of delight now – Les did love his hi-tech gadgets.

Her mind leaped back to the present as her gaze rested on the letters of a large sign.

"But this is Fountains Hall, Les," she said as he turned in through the great iron-railed gates and drove down the stately straight driveway to the white Georgian mansion ahead.

"I managed to reserve a table for us for lunch."

"You're full of surprises this weekend, Les."

"Because you're worth it." He winked her way.

Ten minutes later, as they walked down the corridor to the restaurant she could see ahead, Les stopped her.

"Not that way. Through here." He pushed a door open and sent her in with a hand on her back.

She was instantly greeted by a high cheer from a great crowd, which made her stagger backwards into Les's arms. A host of faces were grinning at her. Faces she recognised. Family faces.

"Happy golden wedding anniversary, Mum." Julie stepped forward and gave her a big hug and kiss, setting a bouquet of roses in shades of gold in her arms.

"We got you them!" her two granddaughters cried, jumping around in front of her, fair curls bobbing.

Julie took her arm and drew her into a crush of family and friends, all wanting to congratulate them with a hug or kiss. Les stood by her, protective as always, accepting handshakes and pats on the back. Someone passed them each a glass of champagne, and Joyce, recovering from the shock, began to enjoy herself.

They spent two hours talking to the guests and thanking them for presents. Then, as everyone found their seats at the arrangement of round tables, Joyce and Les and the immediate family filed along the lengthy top table. It was set out in white and gold with sparkling accessories, just like the room's majestic décor.

"You OK?" Les asked, squeezing her hand.

She nodded, emotion still gripping her throat as she gazed over the guests, still unable to understand how they'd kept this so secret from her.

"Yes, but I still don't understand. I overheard you and Julie arranging the party for next weekend."

Les laughed.

"I wanted you to hear! It was all a ruse to stop you going on about booking this party. You just wouldn't let up. How are we supposed to set up a surprise party when you always want to be in charge?"

"Oh, Les, I'm sorry! And there was I, worried you'd be suspicious that I wasn't going on at you any longer about booking it!"

Glasses tinkled loudly as everybody tapped them with their cutlery. It was a sign for them to kiss, a modern idea which meant that every time the glasses rang out the bride and groom must kiss.

They did so, raising the roof with cheers. Fifty years on, Joyce still felt like a newlywed, still happy to allow Les to make the decisions and take the worry of life away. Especially if it meant surprises like this. ▰

Here Comes The Rain

A S weather predictors go, poor old St Swithin is one of the less reliable. Legend has it that the saint asked to be buried where the rain could fall on his grave, but instead he was placed in a chapel. His displeasure was made plain when it rained solidly for the next 40 days and nights. Thereafter, it was thought if it rained on the saint's day – July 15 – it would continue to do so for the next 40 days. There's no evidence that this has ever happened.

If you want to know if it will rain in the next few hours, have a look at the animals around you. Is your cat washing her ears vigorously? Are the sheep congregating together and coming down from the hills? Have the cows turned their tails into the oncoming wind? These are all said to be signs of impending rain.

However, you can put the brolly away if you see blackbirds singing from the rooftops and higher branches of trees, or if you spot bats and swallows feeding high up late in the evening. High pressure, which brings fine summer weather, means clear skies with little or no wind. Insects fly high then, so the swallows and bats fly higher to catch them. ●

iStock.

Home Truths

by Pat Posner.

Illustration by Michael Thomas.

W OULDN'T it be less drastic just to buy a light therapy lamp, Robbie?" Claire asked the second he opened the front door.

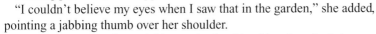

Pushing past him, she stepped inside.

"I couldn't believe my eyes when I saw that in the garden," she added, pointing a jabbing thumb over her shoulder.

Robbie closed the door, sighing at the fact his older sister had chosen today to drive over 100 miles to pay him a surprise visit.

If only she'd come yesterday instead, then he wouldn't have been faced with explaining anything yet.

"I guessed there was something you weren't telling me when you came to see us on Saturday," Claire continued, frowning. "I can't understand why you didn't mention it instead of just going ahead."

"Probably because I knew what your reaction would be. But I don't need a light therapy lamp, Claire. I'm not suffering from winter blues. If anything was drastic it was me moving here after the divorce."

No, leaving Whitwell hadn't been a mistake. He couldn't have stayed in the village with the chance of seeing his ex-wife with her new man. The mistake had been moving so far away from family and friends.

He'd been here long enough now to know he couldn't settle. That was why he'd put the house up for sale – even though it wasn't just any house.

"But you came back to our childhood home!" Claire protested.

"It's been over twenty years since we lived here. Adult experiences don't match up to teenage memories."

"We weren't teenagers when we came for that wedding – Maria James, wasn't it? When the couple living here let us come in and look around, we both said no other house had ever matched up to it for atmosphere and homeliness."

"Yours is cosy and homely, Claire."

"I hope so. Somehow, though, this one beats it." Claire shook her head. "I don't know how a Seventies mid-terraced townhouse can do that, but it does."

"You're right. The house hasn't changed. The area has, though, Claire. Most of the things we remembered aren't here now. Apart from Mrs James next door, there isn't one family on Cottington Close who lived here when we did."

That wasn't surprising. The houses on Cottington Close hadn't long been built when his parents had come to live here as newly-weds. All the neighbours had been around the same age as them, and all had subsequently moved on.

"The house is still here, though, and if it doesn't seem quite as it did when we lived here, it's because it's too masculine," Claire decided. "But you can still feel the atmosphere, and it's still full of happy memories."

That, Robbie thought, watching as his sister stared out of the window at the *For Sale* board in the garden, was probably why she didn't want him to sell it.

"I think memories must mean more to women than to men," Claire said.

"I think they get more emotional about them." Robbie smiled.

His sister had eighteen years' worth of memories here. After they'd moved away, she'd only stayed at home for a couple of years. Even though they'd both ended up just a few miles away from their parents, Robbie guessed that some of Claire's happiest times with them had been here in this house.

"I really cherish my memories," Claire went on, smiling back at him. "Mrs James said that was obvious when she saw us at the funerals."

Mrs James and their mother had kept in touch over the years. It was at their father's funeral that Mrs James had mentioned the house being for sale.

A few months later, after his mother, too, had passed on, Robbie was newly divorced and needing to move, so he had looked online to see if No. 8 Cottington Close was still on the market.

He could see the area around it had changed. The hospital where his mother had worked was no longer there, mills had been demolished or converted into apartments and there was a supermarket where the cinema had been. But he hadn't thought that mattered. It had just seemed like he was meant to buy it.

Turning from the window now, Claire reminded him of that.

"You said it would be your haven."

"It was an emotional decision made when I was at low ebb. My divorce had cut me up. I was in no fit state to think things through properly."

"I suppose it was selfish reasons that made me agree it would be a good move for you," Claire admitted. "I thought it would be great for me to be able to revisit my memories. Sorry."

"I forgive you," Robbie said.

Claire gave him a quick hug.

"But before I agree that you moving back to Whitwell could be good, I want you to be sure you've thought things through," she said. "I doubt you'll get much more than what you paid for the house. With all the fees and removal costs, you could be out of pocket."

Robbie knew that. But he'd be willing to take a small loss if it meant living back where he had friends and family.

"In one way, it's a shame you work from home," Claire said. "It makes moving too easy."

"Working from home is the reason I feel I need to retrace my steps and move back, Claire. Not seeing anyone during the day didn't matter before. I had you, Paul and the kids to pop in on, friends I could meet up with in the evening, or I'd run into someone I knew in the pub." Though, at the time, that had been the problem – he'd kept running into his ex-wife.

"You could go to a pub here, Robbie. You'd soon get to know folk."

"If I go anywhere, I don't seem to fit in. When I see the neighbours, we talk about the weather. But that's all. Perhaps it's because they're all couples or families. Whatever the reason, I feel like an alien and I can't see that changing."

"It would if you had someone new in your life."

Robbie sighed.

"It isn't through lack of trying. I've had dates, but none of them came to anything. That's another reason for wanting to go back to where I know people: friends who'd like to play match-maker. One of them might just succeed."

"What about your main reason for leaving the village? Rowan is still around, you know. And she's still with Doug," Claire reminded him.

"Rowan's ancient history now. I'm over her, Claire."

Claire sighed.

"I can see you've thought it through. I suppose it would be nice having you living close by again. Paul and I would never be stuck for a baby-sitter, either. So let's make a list of what you need to do to make the house look its best."

THE next day, following his sister's advice, Robbie went out and bought new scatter cushions in a warm red colour for his sofa and armchairs. He got herbs in pots for the kitchen window-ledge, a new toaster and matching kettle to stand on the worktop. He'd drawn the line at buying a plug-in thing that supposedly gave off an aroma of fresh bread baking, but he put vases of lavender in the living-room, the spare bedroom and the bathroom. The third bedroom he used for his office and, as he'd told Claire, was off limits.

That afternoon, as Robbie wandered around the house checking the new additions, his phone rang. It was the estate agency asking if one of their sales negotiators could bring a Miss Craig to view the house at three o'clock. It was only 20 minutes' notice, but Robbie willingly agreed.

He sent Claire a text.

Estate agent bringing Miss Craig to view at 3 p.m. Keep your fingers crossed.

It wasn't long before Robbie saw two cars pull up outside.

He had to hide a smile as he wondered what the neighbours would think of him letting in two very attractive women. As neither of them was the one who'd come to do the valuation, Robbie didn't know who was who until the sales negotiator introduced herself as Nicola, and the brunette as Miss Craig.

Miss Craig, who insisted he call her Lizzie, was lively, bubbly and chatty, and suited the brightly coloured slouch beanie hat she wore over her dark, curly hair. Brown eyes sparkling, she admired the pewter duck on the hall table, rubbing a red-gloved finger over its beak.

"As I told Miss Edwards," she began, "my sister and I have a specialist cheese stall on Ashwick market. I live with her at the moment. But now we're opening another stall on the market here. I'll be running it and I want a house within easy travelling distance."

"I live just over the hill," Miss Edwards told her. "I go to the flea market on my Sundays off and it takes me twenty minutes to drive there. It would probably take around ten from here."

Robbie agreed.

"I'm sure a specialist cheese stall will be successful, Miss Craig . . . er, Lizzie."

"You like cheese?" Lizzie asked, dimpling. "You'll have to come to my opening day," she continued. "I'll make sure you get some nice samples.

"I'll also be running my catering business from home," she added, turning to the business in hand. "So I need to have a good look at the kitchen, Mr Howard, before seeing any other rooms."

Robbie led the way. It only took a few minutes for Lizzie to turn an apologetic face to him.

"I knew it wasn't huge from the measurements given on the sales brochure," she said. "There could have been the possibility of switching things around so the 'powers that be' would have approved the design and layout. But I think switching anything around here would give me less room, not more. I'm sorry for wasting your time," she added, glancing from Robbie to Miss Edwards.

Robbie accepted the apology gracefully and wished her good luck in finding somewhere suitable. He even found himself promising he'd visit the cheese stall in Ashwick soon.

"And I'm sure you'll see plenty of me when your new stall here is up and running," Miss Edwards said.

"I've a better idea," Lizzie replied. "My sister and I are having a cheese and wine party a week on Sunday at a pub near Ashwick. I've got invitation cards with me." She rooted in her huge handbag, pulled out two cards and handed them one each. "Please come, to show I'm forgiven for wasting your time."

"I accept. Thank you." Robbie smiled.

"It's my Sunday off," Miss Edwards told her. "So, thank you, and I accept, too." She turned to look at Robbie.

"Hopefully I'll see you before then, Mr Howard, with someone else wanting a viewing."

Robbie watched them walk down the path. Lizzie turned to give him a wave. As he closed the door, Robbie thought a week on Sunday seemed an age away.

When he went into the kitchen he saw one red woollen glove lying on the work surface. Lizzie would be upset to think she'd lost a 100% cashmere glove.

He glanced at the time. He'd phone Claire first; she'd be anxious to hear how the viewing had gone.

Then he'd drive to the estate agent's and ask for Lizzie's home address.

* * * *

"I'm sorry, but I can't give you her home address," Nicola told him. "I'll post the glove to her and tell her how concerned you were that she shouldn't think she'd lost it."

"Returning the glove wasn't the reason I was hoping you'd be here," Robbie said. "I was wondering if . . . if . . ."

He shook his head. He was so out of practice.

"If what?" she prompted.

"The invitation to the cheese and wine do is for a plus one, and I wondered if you'd be taking anybody? Anybody special, I mean."

"There's nobody special in my life right now, Robbie," she said, smiling.

It was the first time she'd used his name. Even though both she and Lizzie had given theirs at his house, he hadn't mentioned his. Which meant she must have looked it up on their records. It sounded good on her lips.

"In that case, maybe we could go together?" Robbie suggested shyly.

"I'd like that," she replied.

WHEN the Sunday of the cheese and wine party arrived, Robbie and Nicola had already spent any spare time they'd had together. They both knew they'd keep on doing so.

A few weeks later they were on their way to Whitwell to spend the weekend with Claire and her family.

"I'm going to enjoy the expression on Claire's face when I tell her I'm not selling up after all, and that you'll be moving in with me," Robbie said, smiling. "It'll be an 'I told you so' look. She likes you a lot, but I think she likes the house we grew up in even more."

Nicola laughed.

"I love the house, too. And its owner. Besides, I need somewhere to live after Lizzie persuaded me to sell her my place once she saw my kitchen!"

Lizzie had become a good friend, calling in on one or other of them whenever she'd been in the area.

"I think she only decided to buy your house to give us a push in the right direction." Robbie laughed. "I'm sure she likes a love story with a cheesy ending." ■

An Italian Idyll

by Jan Halstead.

L IVVIE covered her ears and tried to concentrate over the excited lunchtime chatter of two girls seated at least four desks away. She was running through a rather thoughtless planning application from people with more money than sense. Why destroy half your garden to build your own gym? Surely gardening was exercise enough, and it came with free fresh air!

She took off her glasses and rubbed her eyes. Was it just her, or had the whole world gone mad?

She lost focus yet again as the other girls tried to include her.

"You'll come, won't you, Livvie? It'll be great."

"That depends," Livvie said, giving up any attempt to clear her backlog, "on where and what for."

"Come and see. Steph and I are planning a little holiday," Megan said. "I've got it up online – look. Late deals on the Costa Del Sunshine. Call it a last hurrah before the season of mists and mellow fruitfulness sets in."

"I like the sound of that," Livvie said wistfully.

"Great!" Megan said. "We'll count you in. It's just what you need. You can't fret for ever over one misjudged romance."

Livvie pulled a face.

"No, not the holiday. I meant the mists and mellow fruitfulness. It sounds . . . restful, somehow. I don't think I'm in the mood for the Costas right now."

"Oh, go on," Steph said. "You'll love it when you get there. At least have a look."

Livvie wandered over to look at Megan's computer. Council records had been temporarily replaced with a full-screen Spanish panorama.

From a cloudless blue sky the sun beat down upon a toothpaste white but otherwise faceless tourist hotel. Crowds of sunbeds stretched away into the distance.

"How do you even know it's Spain?" Livvie argued. "This could be anywhere! Look at all the people on that beach. You can scarcely put a pin between them."

"Exactly," Megan agreed. "And you only need one of those people to be Mr Right. I'd say the odds are in your favour!"

Livvie grinned.

"Sorry, but no thanks. I'm not looking for Mr Anything any more; I'm fine on

Illustration by Jim Dewar/iStock.

my own. But you two should go. Press the *Book Now* button and enjoy yourselves. Anyway, in case you've forgotten, we can't all take leave at the same time."

She was right, of course, and the girls gave in, but the conversation left her unsettled. Livvie missed Matt, in spite of everything, and she was feeling disenchanted with her job, so the idea of an autumn break was appealing.

But not the Costas, and definitely no romance! She needed some time to herself.

After all, she had three weeks' holiday owing, and there was no reason not to, once the other girls came back.

She pondered.

What about Italy? Not the north – too frantic at any time of year. Way down south, maybe, the hills.

That could be just the thing.

SIGNOR and Signora Messina matched perfectly their small family-run hotel, which was old with great charm. The few other guests were mostly Italians taking a few days out from the frenzy of city life. And who could blame them?

Livvie had chosen this place with care, not for the things it did have but for the things it didn't – WiFi, disco and coachloads of tourists.

It was rustic and off the beaten track, and cascades of pink bougainvillea tumbled haphazardly over her balcony. Livvie had found the place on her own, struggling somewhat with her next-to-non-existent Italian, but the locals were warm and welcoming and she felt instantly at ease.

And I have three weeks, she thought happily the first morning.

She jumped out of bed and threw open the shutters, startling a small gecko that had been sunning itself on the sill, so that it flicked its tail at her and scuttled away rapidly.

From somewhere below her the clatter of pans rang out and the aroma of fresh Italian coffee rose. She showered quickly and hurried downstairs.

The doors in the dining-room were open to the cool morning breeze so she helped herself to bread, mozzarella and some fruit, and made her way out on to the terrace where tables were set for breakfast. Below them, the hills fell away towards the mist-enshrouded sea.

Livvie smiled shyly at the other guests and wished them a self-conscious *buongiorno* before taking a seat in the corner.

A waiter approached her table.

"*Buongiorno, signorina. Caffè* for you? Cappuccino?"

She ordered cappuccino and he was back within seconds.

He smiled.

"Is beautiful day, no?"

"Yes," Livvie said, relieved that he spoke English, "and I mean to make the most of it. I'm a little stiff from all the travelling yesterday, so I really feel I want to walk. Explore a little, maybe."

The waiter nodded.

"Is good. No rain today. You can walk the estate – up the hill, behind the hotel. We have vines, olives. Is family estate; all our land. Very safe. No get lost."

He gestured out towards the front of the hotel and she could see where the path led away from the front drive and off into the distance.

Livvie considered the phrase "our land". She had taken him for staff.

"So, you are . . .?"

"Arturo. I am Arturo."

There was a summons from another table.

"*Mi scusi.*" He went to answer it.

A lazy wander around the olive groves was just the thing for her first day, Livvie decided. Not to mention the perfect antidote to too much time behind an office desk!

After breakfast she took the route she had been shown, along the dusty road and up the hill.

She was ever so slightly breathless as she headed up past the vineyards to where the olive trees stood, gnarled and bent and heavy with fruit. A cool breeze whipped her hair and she stopped and took deep breaths. Beyond the olive groves the land fell away to the sea, but behind her, inland, the houses clustered together on the hilltops, small villages with narrow lanes, a church and a market square, perhaps.

Everything was much as it had been for hundreds of years. It was, Livvie decided, perfect.

She thought of Matt. They might have shared this. But what would he have made of it? Where she saw a romantic idyll filled with character and tradition, he would have seen potential and profit. He would want to clear things away to make room for modern apartment blocks and tourist bars. The scenery would still be there, but the place would have lost its soul.

They had been right to part. She had never been more certain, and she felt lighter somehow for knowing it.

The path went higher still, leading Livvie away from the cultivated area and up towards the forest. The sea disappeared even further below. Small animals scuttled in the long grass, birds and geckos mostly, darting quickly away as she disturbed them, making her own heart beat a little faster each time.

At the highest point she found she had reached the perimeter of the estate and decided to turn back. She spun on her heel and, as she did so, there was a swishing sound at her feet. She let out a startled shriek as something slim and black disappeared rapidly into the bushes.

She stood for a moment, not wanting to step forward or back, and was scarcely aware of footsteps pounding up the hill towards her.

Arturo appeared suddenly.

"*Signorina*! Something happen? You are all right?"

"S-snake!" she stammered.

She pointed into the bushes and he turned to look.

"Ah! *Serpente nero*. No problem. Nothing poisonous. You scare him."

He laid a reassuring arm tentatively around her shaking shoulder.

"*I* scared *him*?"

Unsure whether to laugh or cry, Livvie was mortified to find tears coming suddenly to her eyes.

"Is the shock," Arturo said. "We go down. We sit."

He steered her gently down the hill to where the olive groves opened out again, and sat her down on an old wooden bench.

"I'm sorry," Livvie said, feeling calmer now. "It wasn't really the snake. Poor thing, I nearly stood on him. I think I've been a bit tense lately, and it's so beautiful here. You know how sometimes you really need a holiday, and then when you get there . . ."

"Is all too much, *signorina*?"

"Yes. All too much. My name is Livvie, by the way.

"Livvie?" he repeated, testing it out.

"Yes. Short for Olivia."

"Ah! Like *oliva*, on the trees. Very special. You speak Italian?"

"Alas, no."

"You need more time here."

He stood up, jumped and made a grab for the nearest tree. He opened his hand. Three plump shiny olives sat there, black and smooth like satin yet still with their green tinge.

"Almost there, but if they drop, they spoil. We begin harvest soon. All the village come. You help. Learn Italian."

He paused and spread his hands apologetically.

"*Mi scusi*. If you want."

He had the most enormous brown eyes, warm and expressive . . .

She looked away. What was she doing? It was this place – the gentle breeze, the ocean, the sights and sounds and scent of it all. Arturo had caught her off guard, and somehow breached whatever emotional defences she'd thought she had built up.

She had given herself a good talking-to after Matt, and was now officially immune to male charm!

"I'll think about it," she said, standing up. "I should go back now. You've been very kind, but you probably have work to do, and I need some coffee. For the shock," she added as an afterthought.

She set off down the road, careful not to look back in case Arturo was watching . . . and in case he wasn't.

THE next few days drifted by lazily. Livvie walked, swam and, on the one day a shower pattered gently on the terrace, retreated to her room with a book. She saw Arturo at breakfast in the mornings, but he did not mention the olives again.

At other times he would be out on the estate. He seemed always to be working but, if he saw her in the gardens, he would stop to chat and point things out to her: butterflies, local herbs and ancient roses, heavy with perfume. He was friendly.

At the weekend the number of residents in the hotel suddenly increased and three people Livvie had not seen before appeared at breakfast. The two men wore smartly tailored suits and the woman, she decided, was more fashion house than olive groves.

They called her Claudia.

Livvie watched as Arturo served them coffee. He seemed to know them well, and they chatted amiably in Italian. Livvie noted how the woman's gaze

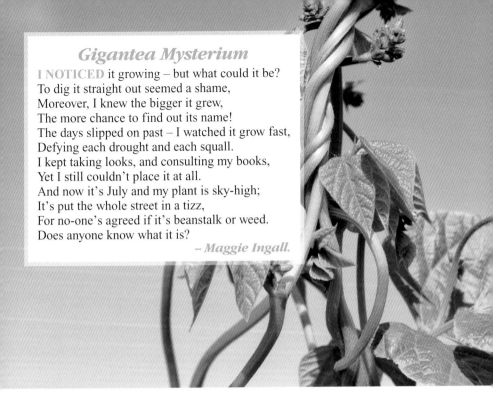

Gigantea Mysterium

I NOTICED it growing – but what could it be?
To dig it straight out seemed a shame,
Moreover, I knew the bigger it grew,
The more chance to find out its name!
The days slipped on past – I watched it grow fast,
Defying each drought and each squall.
I kept taking looks, and consulting my books,
Yet I still couldn't place it at all.
And now it's July and my plant is sky-high;
It's put the whole street in a tizz,
For no-one's agreed if it's beanstalk or weed.
Does anyone know what it is?

– *Maggie Ingall.*

flickered from his face to his strong brown hands. She laughed at something and touched his arm.

Livvie didn't need to speak Italian to know flirting when she saw it. A knot formed in her stomach and she pushed her coffee away.

Arturo turned as she made to leave.

"*Signorina*." He corrected himself. "Livvie, the olives. Tomorrow we begin." She gave him a watery smile.

"I . . ." She was going to say she didn't have time, but that wasn't true and the words wouldn't come. The group at the other table were looking at her now, and suddenly it seemed difficult to refuse.

"I'd love to help."

*   *   *   *

The next day dawned bright and sunny, and as Livvie made her way down the dusty path to the olive groves she found that ahead of her a smattering of villagers, friends and family had already gathered. There were older people, *nonnas* in black, men in flat caps such as her grandad had worn, and families with their children.

Arturo was already there, and he greeted her warmly.

"Thank you for coming, Livvie. We begin, as you see." He waved towards a

iStock.

small boy already sitting in a tree. "You can climb like Filippo, or we have ladders."

The olive trees were short, gnarled and wizened, not beautiful but somehow reminiscent of something from a fairy tale.

An enchanted forest, Livvie thought. And she was in it!

"Stay with me," Arturo said, "and I show you."

She watched as people began to lay nets under the trees, then climbed up by whatever means and slid the olives gently from the branches to be collected in the nets below.

She decided, following Arturo's example, to climb a tree as Filippo had done. The work was tiring but not difficult, and as they picked, chatted and laughed the stresses of home seemed a million miles away.

Arturo, it transpired, was the Messinas' son. This was his home and his livelihood. Among the gathering, Livvie was surprised to see the two businessmen from the day before, dressed down now, stripping olives and blending in seamlessly with the more rustic company.

There was no sign of Claudia.

Livvie nudged Arturo.

"Aren't they . . .?"

"My cousins from the city. They come every year. Everybody help. This is not work, you understand. Nobody paid. The reward is to be here in this beautiful countryside, with your friends, your neighbours. And is better for the olives. Make better oil. Not so good with machine. We are more gentle."

Later, in the heat of the day, they all sat down in the shade of the olive trees and lunch appeared as if by magic. All around her baskets were unpacked and cured meats, cheese, delicious home-baked bread and local wine were shared around.

Livvie sipped her wine and closed her eyes for a moment. She felt a little light-headed.

It had been a long time since she had felt so content.

"Is good to see the smile," Arturo said.

Livvie opened her eyes.

"Don't I smile?"

"Not so much." He seemed to consider whether to say something else. "You look always alone."

There was a look of such concern on his face that she felt compelled to explain.

"There is – was – someone. His name is Matt and he's a property developer. I work in the local planning office. That's how we met and, in a way, that's why we parted."

Arturo nodded encouragingly but didn't interrupt, and Livvie continued.

"There's not much to tell, really. After a while I came to suspect that one of the things he found most appealing about me was my job."

Arturo raised an eyebrow, and Livvie sighed.

"There were advantages to dating someone in the planning office if you were trying to have something approved that was likely to divide opinion."

"I understand," Arturo said.

"I missed him at first," she went on, "but we were very different people. I can see that now. And principles are important, aren't they?"

"They are everything," he said quietly. "But I have made you sad. I am sorry."

He stood up and grabbed hold of the nearest olive branch.

"You see this? Is very important symbol of peace. While you are here, you must put things to rest. Be happy."

She smiled, thinking it would be easy to be happy with him, then blushed as though he might read her mind.

Later, as the last of the sun began to slip below the horizon, they made their way slowly back down to the hotel. They walked in amiable silence, broken only by the sound of the cicadas in the brush.

At the hotel doorway he took her right hand in his and pressed it to his lips.

"Thank you for your help. You will sleep well, I think."

"I hope so."

She did sleep well, and dreamed she was walking through the olive groves.

On one side of her Arturo was gathering olives into the nets.

On the other, Matt was cutting down the trees . . .

LIVVIE awoke with a new certainty. Not only did she not belong with Matt, she did not belong in an office. She wanted something different; a new life.

Arturo failed to appear at breakfast the next day, and Livvie felt a pang of disappointment. She tucked herself away in a little niche in the terraced gardens with a book, but found herself reading the same sentence several times over. The Nordic hero of her novel kept morphing into a tousle-haired Mediterranean one with eyes you could get lost in.

She gave up the attempt when she heard voices drifting up from the terraces below. They were speaking Italian, but she recognised Arturo's voice.

She peeped over the top. It was him and Claudia. They seemed quite animated and there was a lot of arm waving.

Arturo looked angry, but Claudia was smiling coquettishly and stroking his arm as if trying to win him round. In any language it looked like a lovers' tiff.

Livvie turned away, her eyes filling with tears. This was what happened when you eavesdropped on other people.

It was none of her concern.

But it was. Despite all her good intentions she had fallen victim to that most unreliable of things – the holiday romance. It wasn't even really that, was it? It was all in her head.

Suddenly she wanted to be anywhere but where she was. She wished she had never come.

She gathered up her things and stood up to go back to her room, but stopped in her tracks when she saw Arturo standing at the entrance to the arbour looking in at her. She had to go around him; there was no other way out.

"No smile today, Livvie?"

Livvie felt her face redden.

"I'm sorry. I think I'm a little under the weather. I might go and . . ."

She pushed past him, back up the steps to her room. She closed the door behind her and stood with her back to it.

Then she dragged out her suitcase and began to pack. She could not stay here now. Everything was spoiled.

She phoned down to reception and explained that she had to leave the next day, and would they please book her a taxi to the airport.

THE next day, when she paid her bill, it was with a heavy heart that she struggled to reassure the Messinas that there was nothing more they could have done to make her welcome.

She asked how long her taxi would be, but the *signora* would have none of it.

"You will be late. Arturo will take you."

"Oh! But . . ." Livvie stopped as Arturo appeared. She had said nothing to him. What must he think of her?

He wished her his usual *buongiorno* and picked up her case. She followed him out to the car. As they pulled away, she looked back up the hill towards the olive groves and swallowed.

"I didn't mean for you to have to take me," she said eventually.

"Is no trouble," he said quietly. "You are sick, perhaps, for England?"

"Sick? Oh, homesick, you mean. Pining." She looked away from him, her face set. "Something like that."

With that, conversation came to a halt.

As the airport came into view Arturo pulled into the drop-off area and turned off the ignition, then climbed out to fetch her luggage from the boot.

He gave a wan smile.

"I must wish you safe journey."

"Thank you, Arturo, for everything. I've had a wonderful time and you've all been very kind."

This wasn't easy.

"Forgive me, I overheard you yesterday. I hope you can sort things out with Claudia. Offer the olive branch, as you would say."

He looked puzzled.

"You understand what we were saying?"

"Well, no. Not really." But it had been obvious, hadn't it?

He looked at his watch.

"We sit." With that he opened the car door again. "Please."

Reluctant as she was to drag things out, Livvie climbed back into the car. He took her hand in his.

"Claudia and I are at university together. I study environment; she is business student. Now I am home, where I belong. Is all natural. Beautiful. What I love. Now Claudia is working for big tourist company. They want to buy. I say no. So now Claudia is also going home."

His eyes fixed on hers.

"Your principles are everything. Is right?"

"Yes," Livvie said. "But if you love her . . ."

His eyes widened, then he threw back his head and laughed.

"Love? Claudia? No, no! I am not sick for Claudia like you are sick for . . ." He frowned, trying to remember. "Matt!"

You didn't have to be Italian to be dramatic. Livvie widened her own eyes and gave a contemptuous look.

"Love? Matt? Me?"

He'd stopped laughing.

"But you go back to England to Matt. You are heartsick."

Livvie felt suddenly breathless.

"Homesick? I'm not homesick. Quite the opposite. I'm more at home here than I could ever have imagined. All this, what you do here – it all makes sense to me."

She dropped her gaze.

"And you, Arturo. You make sense to me."

He gripped her hand more tightly.

"Because we are the same," he said. "You must stay, Livvie. Please. Finish your holiday, and you will see."

He raised a finger and broke into a smile.

"Also, for next week Filippo's father has many olive trees."

Livvie knew what came next.

"Everybody help. You come. Learn Italian."

Arturo spread his hands apologetically just as he had that first day.

"*Mi scusi*. If you want."

"I want," Livvie said, laughing out loud. "I really, really want!"

And to seal the deal she let herself be kissed on both cheeks and then, very gently, on the mouth.

Arturo turned the car around and took her back. Back to a different kind of life.

Livvie would need to sort things out at home. It would take some planning. But it was a start, and after all, Livvie knew all about planning. ■

Bo'ness, Scotland

BO'NESS, or Borrowstounness, can be traced back to Roman times when it is believed to have formed the eastern end of the Antonine Wall, the northernmost border of the Roman Empire. You can still find traces of the wall today in the centre of the town, and it's now known locally as Graham's Dyke.

Bo'ness was a major port on the Firth of Forth and a centre of heavy industry in the 18th century, and glimpses of the past can still be seen today on the preserved Bo'ness-Kinneil Railway. Steam trains run for three miles along the shores of the Forth from Bo'ness to the Fireclay Mines at Birkhill. You can take a real trip into the past by going on a guided tour of the underground workings. Look out for the railway's specially themed days, too – their "Thomas The Tank Engine Day" is always very popular.

Only 16 miles north-west of Edinburgh and six miles east of Falkirk, this historic town is also perfectly situated to let you enjoy nearby attractions such as the Falkirk Wheel, Callendar House and the Kelpies. ■

Illustration by André Leonard.

Share, And Share Alike

by Valerie Bowes.

ON'T they look young?" Doreen gazed fondly at the photo. "Which is Great-grandma, Nanna?" Kerry leaned closer. "That's her." Doreen set her finger on the girl with fair, wavy hair. "That's my mum, Molly. That's little Joy in the middle, and that's Pat."

The three girls looked back at her, faded by time but still brimming with hope and vitality. Molly on the left was plump; Pat on the right was dark-haired and taller. They leaned in, laughing, with the pixie-faced girl between them.

On the back of the photo, in neat handwriting, it said: *Met in wartime, friends for life. 1942.*

* * * *

1942

"Guess what, girls?" Molly flashed her finger and the others gathered round, bouncing with congratulations.

"Well, can't say we didn't see it coming," Pat said. "Talk about stars in the eyes whenever Ted came in!"

"And always wangling an extra scrape of butter for him. Don't think I didn't notice!" Joy hugged her friend.

"It's not Ted," Molly said, shaking her head dejectedly.

"What?" Joy's eyebrows nearly disappeared into her hair. "Who, then?"

"Of course it's Ted!" Pat said. "Haven't you known her long enough to know when she's pulling your leg? There's never been anyone else, has there, Moll?"

There hadn't. Not since the moment he walked into the NAAFI with the rest of the bomber crew.

"Oh, you!" Joy slapped Molly's arm, but her eyes remained troubled.

"What's up, Titch?" Very little got past Pat's notice.

"Isn't it the wrong . . . you know. Should you . . . right now?" Joy didn't know how to put it into words. She didn't want to dampen Molly's happiness.

"You mean, what if he gets shot down?" Molly was always one to face things squarely. "That could happen tomorrow. All the more reason for us to get married while we can."

"Hear, hear," Pat agreed. "When's it going to be? Are we going to be bridesmaids? What are you going to wear?"

And therein lay the rub. Even pooling their clothing coupons left them far short of what they needed. There was no hope of being able to buy something new. Rummaging in their wardrobes only produced a petticoat and a white satin blouse with a stain on one sleeve, and Molly's mother had unearthed a length of pretty lace from a box in the attic.

"I'll wear my pink costume. There is a war on, you know."

"Lucky old men," Pat said. "They'll be in uniform, so it's no problem for them. Don't worry, Molly. Ted will think you're gorgeous whatever you wear."

"If he even notices." Joy sniffed. "I wish I hadn't used all my points for that blue frock. I had to prod Jimmy to tell me if he liked it, and you could see he hadn't even noticed I had something new. How they ever find their way across Germany, I'll never know. Blind as bats, if you ask me."

The matter became urgent when Ted's crew were granted leave. Molly hurried into the NAAFI where Pat was busy making sandwiches.

"Saturday!"

"Saturday?" Pat stared at her, the knife poised over the Spam she was cutting. "But that's only four days away. We'll never be ready."

"Yes, we will. I've already made the cardboard tiers to make the sponge look like a wedding cake. I'll wear my pink. Joy's got that new frock and you've got a blue one as well, so at least you'll match."

The door banged open and Joy barged in, almost hidden by a large, unwieldy parcel.

"Look what I've got!" She gasped. "Can you do something with this, Molly?"

The parcel was torn open by eager fingers.

"Oh!" Molly stared at the billowing material. "Where on earth did you get it?"

"From Ethel in Packing. It's no use as a parachute any more. Got a great big tear in it, see?"

Molly dropped the material as if it had burned her fingers.

"No-one candled?" she said apprehensively.

"No, of course not. How would it have got back to Packing if someone hadn't made it?" Joy measured the fabric against her arm. "It was that Scots chap with the glasses. It got torn somehow and he brought it back to get a new one. Don't ask me how it happened – Ethel said he's that clumsy she wasn't surprised."

"He's not clumsy," Pat said hotly. "You should see the beautiful flies he ties. You'd think they were real."

The other girls exchanged gleeful nudges.

"How would you know about his flies?" Molly asked innocently as Joy giggled.

"Oh, you lot!" Pat cast her eyes heavenwards. "For fly-fishing! Anyway, what about this silk? Can we do something with it?"

Of course they could. They'd had plenty of practice with Make Do And Mend. Molly fashioned the parachute silk into a skirt that evening, while Joy tackled the satin blouse. She put in new darts to fit the bodice to Molly's figure, removed the sleeves and replaced them with ones made from the length of lace.

"Look at that! There's enough material in these old sleeves to face the neckline once I've got rid of this ghastly pie-frill collar."

"That'll look a lot better," Molly agreed.

The creamy white of the satin didn't exactly match the white of the parachute, but beggars couldn't be choosers, as Molly stoutly maintained when she paraded the dress for her friend.

"Well, I think it looks lovely on you," Joy said.

"So do I." Pat came in with a triumphant twirl. "And I've got the finishing touch. Borrowed it off that tall WAAF who only got married a couple of weeks ago."

She draped the veil over her head and batted her eyelashes.

"You'll knock Ted's socks off when he sees you coming down that aisle," Joy predicted happily, tweaking the skirt into place.

Ted's aircraft didn't come back to the base on Thursday. Molly's stomach seemed to have vanished with it, leaving an echoing empty void. The next day, her eyes bleared with sleeplessness, she was scraping a minuscule amount of butter on slices of bread when Pat towed the Scots lad into the NAAFI.

"I saw G-George go down," the wireless operator said in his east-coast Scots accent.

Molly clasped her hand over her mouth to keep the wail of anguish in.

Pat caught her arm.

"No, Molls, listen."

"But I saw three or four chutes get away," Duncan added reassuringly.

Three or four out of a crew of seven!

Molly knew they were trying to give her hope, but it didn't feel hopeful to her. Even if one of the figures dangling from those chutes was Ted, he'd have landed somewhere in enemy territory. What would happen to him then?

As if she was watching from above her own head, she saw Pat's fingers twine around Duncan's, and the way her hand nestled into his.

A FTER weeks with no news of G-George's crew, Molly almost found herself wishing that Duncan hadn't told her about the men floating away from the burning plane. To have mourned Ted would have been bad enough; not knowing whether he had jumped from the frying-pan into the fire was torture.

It was made worse by Pat and Duncan's growing closeness. Every time the planes took off, Molly and Joy would be there either side of Pat, listening to them drone away into the dangerous sky, and would stay with her until the dawn brought them back.

"Thank goodness Jimmy's ground crew," Joy murmured to Molly, yawning. "At least there's a few nights we get some sleep."

"We're getting married." Pat's voice wavered between gladness and defiance.

Molly had been pretty sure for quite some time, but she guessed that her friend had been reluctant to tell her, afraid that it would be rubbing it in.

"Oh, that's wonderful, Pat! Congratulations." In her desire to be happy for Pat, she could hear that she was gushing too much. "When?"

"As soon as possible." The loss of G-George hung for a moment in the air. "If we're married and anything happens, I'd be his next of kin. At least I'd be told."

It was so hard for girlfriends of the air crew, when no information could be

There And Back Again

IT'S sad, you'll agree, when a holiday ends.
Farewell to new places, farewell to new friends,
With postcards all posted, and souvenirs stowed,
With cases collected, it's time for the road.
We wave as we're leaving. Goodbye! Oh, goodbye!
Will we go back? We'll certainly try.
We've seen lots of sights and we've seen lots of sun,
With outings and ice-creams, we've surely had fun.
We sigh as we turn, and it all disappears;
Yet isn't it strange, as our house ever nears,
Though lovely it's been to relax and to roam,
There's one thing apparent – it's good to be home.
– Maggie Ingall.

given to them.

"Good," Molly replied, hugging her. "You'll wear the dress, of course?"

"Are you sure?"

"Unless you think it'll bring you bad luck?" Molly hadn't thought of it before, but now she gazed at Pat in consternation.

"Don't be daft. It wasn't the dress's fault that G-George bought it. But we made it for you. Are you sure you want me to wear it?"

"Where would you get another one? Anyway, that dress means something to all of us. It's as much yours and Joy's as mine. We all had a hand in making it."

* * * *

Joy was setting up the Singer while Molly was pinning the bodice to fit Pat, when the door opened and a head appeared round it.

"Telephone call for you, Molly."

"Who's calling at this time of the evening?" Molly said crossly through a mouthful of pins. "If it's the chap saying he's going to be late delivering the rations again, he'll get a piece of my mind."

But when she picked up the phone, it was Ted's mother, incoherent with tears and relief.

"We've just heard – he's in Stalag Luft something or other. It's OK – he's safe, Molly!"

"Oh, thank God!" Molly was too overcome to say much. She listened to Ted's mother telling her the details of where he was and promising to send her the address so she could write to him.

*   *   *   *

"So Pat wore the dress first," Doreen explained, "then little Joy."

"She married Jimmy, then?" Kerry said.

"No, she married Graham. He was a Brown Job. In the Army." Doreen laughed, seeing Kerry's puzzled frown. "A friend of her brother's. He lost an arm at the D-Day landings and was invalided out. The dress got taken in for Pat and shortened for Joy, and let out again when Dad was repatriated at the end of the war."

"So all three of them wore it," Kerry said. She stroked the fragile fabric gently.

"It wasn't unusual, you know. Mum heard of one wedding dress that was worn by fifteen girls! But you won't have to do that. There are whole shops full of lovely dresses. Which one will you choose?"

"None!" Kerry said. She grinned cheerfully at her grandmother. "I don't want one that's just picked off a rail. I want one that means as much as this did to Molly, Pat and Joy."

"But you couldn't wear this," Doreen said, thinking she could see where Kerry was going. "It's been altered so many times, and the parachute silk's discoloured."

"No," Kerry agreed. "I know I can't. But Trish is great at dressmaking, and Sophie says she'll design it. I'd rather have a dress my friends made for me than the most expensive one in any shop."

With sudden inspiration, Doreen lifted the wartime dress from its nest of tissue paper.

"The skirt and bodice can't be worn again, but why don't you take the sleeves? The lace is still good, and I'm sure Trish could use it somewhere."

"Are you sure, Nan? Wouldn't your mum rather you kept it intact?"

Doreen smiled.

"That dress wasn't just made with odds and ends. It was made with love and friendship. Maybe it rubbed off, because they all celebrated their Golden Weddings. They'd be tickled pink to know that part of it was walking down the aisle again."

Kerry picked up the photo.

"I tell you what, we'll frame this and put it in pride of place at the reception."

And Doreen was sure she saw the faces in the photograph beam even wider. ▨

Autumn Leaves

As the days move towards the autumn equinox, the cooler night-times and shorter days begin to break down the green chlorophyll in the leaves of deciduous trees. This leaves behind the glorious yellows, oranges and reds that were masked by the green, making a spectacular display before the leaves finally fall. A dry, bright summer followed by sunny, but not frosty, days in autumn brings the brightest colours.

If the leaves fall from the trees early, it's said that winter will be mild; if they fall late (after Martinmas Day, on November 11), tradition says that winter will be severe.

The quantity of berries and nuts on trees are also said to indicate a harsh winter. When holly is laden with red berries and the oak bountiful with acorns, ready to be stored by busy squirrels, it must mean that nature is preparing for cold days ahead . . . mustn't it?

Well, not really. It seems that all that bounty is more the effect of weather conditions earlier in the year and the squirrels and other critters are merely cashing in on the available bonanza. ●

On Top Of The World

by Mary Kettlewell.

"**M**ISS BLENHEIM."

Kirsteen rose to her feet and entered the interview room. Two men, bearded and wind-burnt, stared at her slight figure. "I'm Alistair Reed, Chief Meteorologist, and this is Fergus Ruan, my assistant. I'll be blunt. Conditions on the summit of Ben Nevis are brutal during the winter. It's too tough a job for a woman."

"I think you are mistaken, Mr Reed. My father came second in the first race to the summit in 1898."

"No mean achievement, but that was your father. Not you."

"True, but I had climbed to the top, at the age of twelve, to watch his victory."

"You didn't hire a pony?"

"No. I went on foot." She gave the men an uncompromising stare.

"Have you ever experienced severe winter conditions?"

"Yes, my late grandfather was a mountaineer. He took me on winter treks in the Cairngorms."

"What experience have you of meteorology?"

"I've studied every book I can get hold of. And I am a fast learner."

"Do your parents approve of your application?"

"Father is a sea captain, abroad most of the time. He is thrilled that I want to follow in my grandfather's footsteps. Mother passed away five years ago."

"I am very sorry to hear that, Miss Blenheim."

Half an hour later she was summoned back into the room.

"We have decided to offer you the post on a trial basis. If we're not satisfied you will go down with the last pony train in three weeks' time when the Summit Hotel closes for winter. We look forward to working with you."

✳   ✳   ✳   ✳

Alistair met her outside a hotel in Fort William and they hitched a ride on a farmer's cart to Glen Nevis. It was late September and both were dressed in windproof clothing and sturdy boots.

"No ponies today, I'm afraid, Miss Blenheim. They are busy taking winter supplies up to the observatory. We'll have to tackle it on foot."

She stared up at the ridge.

"It looks as if we are lucky. No cloud on the summit."

They crossed the bridge over the River Nevis.

"Looking forward to the job?"

"Yes, I am. Once the Summit Hotel packs up for winter I imagine conditions are hard up there."

Illustration by PWA.

"Very. Last year we recorded a temperature of minus-eleven centigrade and twenty feet of snow on the summit plateau."

By now he was striding out fast and Kirsteen knew he was testing her. By the time they reached the steep screes leading to the summit several hours later, she was 20 yards ahead. Later, at the cairn on top, he had the good grace to chuckle.

"You've put me firmly in my place."

She turned a pair of innocent green eyes on him.

"Don't tell me you're tired, Mr Reed. It's been a nice afternoon stroll."

That evening he took her to dine at the Summit Hotel. The Misses Gribben, the two sisters who owned it, were busy packing up ready for their descent. Fergus Ruan, the other meteorologist, joined them. He was a dour Scot with a dry sense of humour.

"Come the winter you'll be wishing you were down in Fort William sampling its delights instead of turning into an icicle up here."

"Not at all, Mr Ruan. And I have no intention of turning into an icicle."

The meal was dished up by Mrs Maclaren, a thin, withered woman who gave her a penetrating stare.

"So, you'll be spending the winter with me in the hotel. I hope you've brought your hot-water bottle." She pursed her lips. "You'll be needing it. My chilblains were wicked last year."

Afterwards, she showed Kirsteen her room and softened.

"It'll be good to have another body close by. It can be lonesome in winter, especially when the men are busy with their measurements."

"Do you always stay up here?"

"For the past three years. And a good job I do! I've had a blizzard blowing open the front door, water trickling into the dining-room and burst pipes. Not to mention the wind howling. Anyway, it wouldn't be proper, you up here on your own with those two weathermen."

"Doesn't your family worry about you?"

"I lost my only sister two years back and the rest emigrated to America."

"You don't feel cut off?"

"I don't mind my own company. My husband loved the mountains. He was a shepherd in Sutherland."

"How did you lose him?"

"He was searching for lambs when a blizzard blew up from nowhere. They found him several days later, frozen, clutching two lambs in his arms. It reminds me of him, being up here."

"I'm sorry. I shouldn't have asked."

"Not at all."

By the time the last ponies arrived Kirsteen had decided.

"I'd like to stay for the winter, Mr Reed."

"We'd like to have you, Miss Blenheim." He put a friendly hand on her shoulder. "And how about dropping the formalities? I'm Alistair."

She smiled.

"Kirsteen."

She left the room feeling she was no longer just an employee. Alistair was treating her as a friend and she was warming to him.

As the beasts plodded off down the snow-covered track, however, loneliness hit her like a brick wall. The bleak, stony summit, and the fearsome black cliffs dropping down to Coire Leis 2,000 feet below, sent a shiver through her.

Alistair must have sensed her uneasiness for he led her over to the tower topping the observatory.

"Do you know the history of the tower? It was erected ten years ago in 1894. The early meteorologists endured some hard winters. They were unable to take measurements and there was a nasty incident. One of them was caught in a snowstorm and couldn't find the entrance."

"How high is it?"

"Thirty feet. It means we can get inside the observatory even when the Ben is at her most vicious. I'd like you to be responsible for the anemometer. We need wind strength measurements four times a day. And we keep a log book of each day's weather. I wonder whether you'd like to take that over."

"Very much, Alistair. What about cooking and cleaning?"

"We all chip in to help Mrs Maclaren at the hotel from time to time. I'm sure she'd appreciate another pair of hands."

That evening she gave Mrs Maclaren help with sorting the hotel bedding.

"It's a strange job for a girl to take on." She gave Kirsteen a look. "Not running away from trouble, are you?"

Kirsteen smiled.

"No, Mrs Maclaren. I just wanted a challenge."

"You'll have it here. There's never a dull moment in the winter. Spiders sheltering from the weather in the bath, ceilings caving in. Why, I've seen the washing freeze solid." She pursed her lips. "And not even a wee drop of whisky to take off the chill. This is a temperance hotel."

"How long have the meteorologists worked here, Mrs Maclaren?"

"Call me Morag, dearie. We'd best be on friendly terms seeing as we're here for the winter. It's Fergus Ruan's first year. He came up in the spring. He's an ex-trawler skipper turned weatherman. Tough as old boots and dry as cinders. But he's got a kindly streak and he's good at his work."

"Alistair Reed used to be an explorer, so I've heard."

"Aye. Expeditions to Greenland and out of the way places like that."

"Is he married?"

"That I couldn't say. He's not one to talk about himself."

Kirsteen wondered. There was no sign of a ring on his finger, but that meant nothing. She dropped off to sleep to the tune of rattling windows, the banshee howl of the ceaseless wind and the banging of a distant door.

∗   ∗   ∗   ∗

They woke to a white-out. Visibility was less than six feet and the air temperature was a bitter minus seven.

"Do you still do the readings in this, Alistair?"

He nodded.

"We never miss, if possible. That's what the lifelines I showed you are for. I'll come with you."

It was the most terrifying walk of her life. Holding the rope in one hand, she followed behind Alistair's spectral figure. Snow crunched under her feet and she was in a desolate, empty world, unable to see, fearful of the precipices that lurked all around. Once, she heard the sound of falling rocks and was grateful when Alistair reached back and touched her gloved hand.

Whilst she took the readings he stood between her and the bitter wind blowing off the north face and she was grateful for the small kindness. When she had taken the readings, he bent close to be heard above the moan of the gale.

"I'm glad you're with us for the winter, Kirsteen. You and Fergus are the best workers I've had."

They returned to the observatory, relief flooding through her when she saw the ice-encased buildings. Inside, Fergus took the pipe from his mouth and grinned.

"Like walking into the gates of hell, isn't it? I froze the first time. Kept thinking I was going to step out into space."

When Fergus left to check the humidity levels, Kirsteen brewed coffee and they sat down by the wood fire. She felt relaxed.

"What made Fergus choose to work up here? Wasn't he happy working on the trawlers?"

"His brother was on the deep-sea boats off Iceland. One winter the trawler got top-heavy with ice and she rolled. His brother was unlucky. He didn't make it."

"How dreadful!"

"Fergus couldn't face the sea after that. I think he finds peace up here." Alistair gave her a long look. "And you, Kirsteen? Why did you choose the mountain? There are other weather stations down below."

She sipped her coffee.

"I suppose I've been looking for peace, too. I was friendly with a newly commissioned officer from one of the Scottish regiments. I fell in love and we got engaged. Then he was posted abroad."

"You never heard from him again?"

She nodded.

"When this job came up I thought, this is for me. I wanted to get away from everything and the Ben was the answer."

"Does it still hurt?" he asked softly.

"Sometimes, in the small hours. But the mountain is proving a wonderful healer."

"Kirsteen, will you walk along the ridge with me tomorrow? We always take it easy on the Sabbath."

"There is something I need to know first. You aren't married or committed to someone down below?"

"No. There is nobody."

"Then, yes, I'd like to come with you."

Kirsteen had just finished her entry in the log when Alistair hurried in.

"Quick, Kirsteen! There's something I want to show you outside. It's very unusual."

He led her to the edge of the plateau. She looked down and gasped. There, on the cloud below, were two huge shadows surrounded by a halo containing all the delicate pastel shades of the rainbow.

"I've never seen anything so beautiful! What is it?"

"A Brocken Spectre and glory. It's the sun casting our shadow on to the clouds." He moved a few steps closer and their outlines merged.

Carnival

IT'S Carnival Day, and spirits are high,
The bunting is up, the sun's in the sky,
The floats are all ready, the streets are all clear,
It's time to begin, so off with a cheer!
Up strikes the band, with pipers and drums,
And then, can I see? Yes, look, here she comes!
The Carnival Queen, with a page boy and maid,
Bashful and beaming, they lead the parade.
The lorries and motors, decked out to impress,
With folks in their finest, or strange fancy dress.
Midst music and mayhem, they move down the street,
The whole town is dancing to Carnival beat!

— *Maggie Ingall.*

"Look," he said quietly. "We've drawn close."

When he put an arm round her she did not draw back, and there was magic in the air when he touched his lips to her cheek. Happiness welled up in her.

✳ ✳ ✳ ✳

The men were out early relaying the safety lines. Mrs Maclaren finished mopping the kitchen floor.

"We'll have a spring clean of their rooms while they're busy, dear. You take Mr Alistair's and I'll do Fergus's."

Kirsteen was dusting the mantelpiece when she saw the photograph. It was of Alistair holding the hand of a bride in white dress and train. They were looking at each other and smiling. Beside it sat an open birthday card.

Alistair, darling, a happy birthday, my love. How I miss you up there on the mountain top.

A row of kisses followed.

It was shock that hit Kirsteen first; shock that he had been dishonest. His words came back to her: "There is nobody."

How could he have told her such an untruth? All the time he had a loving wife waiting for him, yet he had put his arm round her waist and kissed her cheek. What a fool she had been!

Mrs Maclaren found her in tears and patted her arm in a motherly way.

"I'm sorry, dearie. I had no idea. He keeps things to himself. Those things weren't there last time I did his room. What you need is a strong cup of tea."

He came back an hour later.

"Thank you for doing my room, Kirsteen. I'm afraid it was in a mess."

Then he saw the coldness in her face.

"It is a good thing I did. I don't take kindly to being led up the garden path."

He looked shocked.

"What are you talking about?"

"The photograph and birthday card."

"No!" His voice sounded strangled, hurt. "You have it all wrong."

"You told me you weren't married!"

"I wanted to tell you," he replied brokenly. "But I couldn't. The fact is, both of us were climbing enthusiasts. We were tackling a face in Wales. Petra was leading and I was following her up. A piton broke loose. She didn't have a chance. We had only been married six months. The birthday card was the last thing she gave me."

He was crying openly now and Kirsteen put her arms round him, holding him tightly.

"Alistair, I am so deeply sorry for what I said. Please forgive me."

"There's nothing to forgive, Kirsteen. You couldn't have known. I want to tell you something. That day we climbed the Ben for the first time you teased me about getting to the summit first, and we both laughed. I hadn't done that for months. And you smiled at me over our first meal with Fergus and Mrs Maclaren. That was when I started to find hope again. It was like seeing a speck of light at the end of a dark tunnel. Go on holding me, Kirsteen."

She did and a warmth enfolded them and she didn't want to let him go. Then came Mrs Maclaren's voice.

"Well, now, I think we could all do with a cup of coffee and some home-made biscuits after all that sadness." She leaned over and gave Alistair a kiss on the cheek. "It's that sorry I am to hear of your grieving, Mr Alistair." She glanced at Kirsteen. "I'm thinking that maybe things will be better for you now."

✶   ✶   ✶   ✶

Winter set in with a vengeance, hostile and hard. Packed snow drifted against the observatory tower, turning it into a glacial wedding cake of icicles. Ben Nevis, "the mountain with its head in the clouds", was showing its cruel side.

The thermometer registered a bitter minus fifteen degrees outside. Inside the warmth of the observatory Kirsteen was cooking a breakfast of bacon and eggs while Fergus did some repairs to the spare compasses. Alistair had ventured out to take the humidity reading.

"He should be back by now," she said, glancing at the clock.

"Don't worry. He'll be fumbling with frozen fingers."

Five minutes passed.

"I'm going to check that he's all right."

"Not on your own, you're not. I'll come with you. But I tell you this, Alistair is a born survivor."

She followed Fergus over the glazed ice and the air caught roughly at her throat. A line of indentations led to the anemometer. Then, to her horror, she saw that a great slab of snow had broken away above the precipice.

Suddenly the air fragmented with a desperate cry.

"Help! I am in deep trouble."

Stepping gingerly forward, Fergus and Kirsteen peered down the fearsome depths of the north face. They couldn't see Alistair because of an overhang.

"Where are you, Alistair?" Fergus's voice was rock steady.

"On a narrow ledge below the outcrop," the reply came. "I've twisted my ankle."

Kirsteen was already running back towards the observatory for a rope. Two minutes passed, three, maybe four. She came back, white-faced and panting, the coil of rope slung over her shoulder and an ice axe and pitons dangling from her hand.

"I can't hold on much longer! The ledge is crumbling." Alistair's voice held an edge of panic.

Within seconds Fergus had hammered in a piton and slung the rope over the cliff.

"I can't reach it, Fergus! The rope is too far out!"

"Hang on for dear life. I'm coming down."

"No, Fergus." Kirsteen's voice was urgent. "I won't be strong enough to pull you up. I'm the one who must go down."

"You can't! It's too dangerous."

She ignored him.

"Take the rope and keep it taut."

Before he could reply she had lowered her legs over the void. Sick with fear, she inched her way down, hand over hand, staring at the glittering ice and sharp points of rock. What lay below was too terrible to contemplate.

Then a hand grasped her ankle.

"Kirsteen, for the love of God don't come down any further! The ledge is going."

"Grab the rope end, Alistair. I'll climb back and we'll pull you up." Like a flat spider, she eased her way upwards, scrabbling for footholds. A chunk of snow gave and she nearly fell. Then Fergus reached down, caught her arm, dragged her clear of the drop and thrust her back.

Winding the rope round their waists, both he and Kirsteen leaned back with all their weight. Her breath was bursting in her lungs, her arms on fire.

Then Alistair's head appeared and he emerged from the abyss. One either side of him, his arms round their shoulders, they got him back to the observatory. He had an injured ankle but, it appeared, little else.

Mrs Maclaren had already unearthed a bottle of whisky from the secret store and had poured them out generous measures.

Fergus shook his head at Kirsteen.

"You're crazy, lass! Lowering yourself down into that hell!" He gave a thin smile. "It's a pity we haven't got more women up here. They outshine the men every time."

Then it was Alistair's turn to speak.

"I owe my life to you, Kirsteen. I thought I was about to meet my maker. You are the bravest person I've ever met and I love you beyond measure."

Mrs Maclaren took a sip at her whisky.

"I don't know – we women turn our heads for one minute and you men are in trouble. What would they do without us, Kirsteen? Fall off cliffs, freeze to death and end up buried in snow drifts, like as not." She pointed to Alistair. "You'd best see to that foot of his. I'll get a nice warming stew on the go." Then her voice softened and she gave Kirsteen a hug. "Thank the Lord you are safe, child. I was worried out of my mind."

Over that winter their love grew. Slowly the tendons in Alistair's ankle healed and it was a very special day when he went outside and limped over to the rain gauge, his hand holding Kirsteen's tightly. They celebrated it with a kiss.

By the end of April the first line of ponies had reached the summit with provisions. Two relief weathermen came to replace Alistair and Kirsteen, who were due a well-earned month's vacation. Mrs Maclaren was to stay with a friend in Ramsgate and Fergus planned to go trout fishing with some of his sailor pals.

Alistair told Kirsteen of his first priority when they descended.

"I want to call in at the jeweller's in Fort William, Kirsteen, my love, to buy an engagement ring. If you will have me, that is."

She kissed his cheek.

"I think you are going to need me around to make sure you don't go tumbling down that north face again next year!"

When she heard the news Mrs Maclaren dabbed at her eyes.

"You can't say you don't get drama on the Ben. Folks falling over cliffs, glories, and now love affairs. Blessings on you both."

Fergus gave one of his thin smiles.

"So you'll be wanting me for best man, will you? Don't expect me to give one of those fancy speeches."

Then he produced a bottle of Scotch, twelve years old this time, and poured out celebratory tots. He raised his glass.

"*Slainte mhòr*! The best of health to ye both." ∎

Roseland, Cornwall

ST JUST IN ROSELAND is a beautiful 13th-century church, with an even older sixth-century Celtic heritage, and is well worth a visit.

Legend has it that Joseph of Arimathea may have brought Jesus ashore here. Whether that's true or not, the church certainly attracts numerous visitors each year and recently underwent restoration works to replace large sections of the roof which had become structurally unsound.

The church is set in a unique waterside semi-tropical garden, with small streams and little bridges throughout the graveyard. Visitors comment on what a serene place it is, with plenty of places simply to sit and think in relaxing surroundings.

Look out for the hidden well and little maps that help you navigate the paths. There's also a café and nearby toilets, so spiritual and physical needs are both well taken care of! ■

Illustration by Sailesh Thakrar.

Saha And The Robin

by Molly Gourlay.

SAHA stood at the kitchen window. It was early in the morning and it was raining again. It always seemed to be raining here.

Everything looked so grey, so dismal, and Saha felt the same dull greyness in her heart. She missed her homeland of India. She missed the warmth, the rich colours and the beauty of the land, and she missed her people. It all seemed so far away now.

She sighed, and then quickly scolded herself.

"You have no need to feel so sad, Saha. You are really very blessed, you know."

She thought fondly of her granddaughter Ada and husband Ragi. They had kindly paid for her to come to Britain so that they could look after her now that she was alone and getting older, and she was very grateful for their care.

Ada and Ragi had tried to make the transition as easy as possible for her, preparing a lovely bedroom with a bright red embroidered quilt and pretty floral curtains. And they had turned the heating up to warm her old bones. Britain was such a cold place!

"I have been told that these trees will have bright green leaves in the spring, and that this little garden will have pretty flowers in the summer," she reminded herself as she looked on to the grey skies and sodden earth. "There will be brightness and warmth in this place, too. It will just take time and I must learn to be patient."

Saha did not know anyone in the street yet. Life was so different here and she felt shy, and sometimes frightened at the strangeness of it all.

In India, life had always been lived outside. There had always been the chattering of family and neighbours as you went about your cooking and your washing; always laughter, always joy, always friendship.

Here, everyone seemed to live in their own little boxes behind closed doors. Of course, the weather no doubt was the main reason for that!

Saha chuckled as she pictured herself trying to cook chapatis and curry in some of the downpours she had witnessed here recently.

It was not that it didn't rain in India. The monsoon rains would have everyone ducking for cover, but at least everyone knew when to expect them. Here, it could be bright one moment, and then bitterly cold or wet the next. Such a strange country.

"Just wait till the summer, Grandmother," Ada had told her. "There will be barbecues every night. We will roast chicken and vegetables on charcoal just like at home."

"The only difference is that you will be clad in a raincoat and wellies, and cooking will be done in a puddle under an enormous umbrella!" her husband had added with a twinkle in his eye.

Ada had scolded him and told him to stop teasing Grandma Saha!

There seemed to be a large number of young families living in the street. Saha enjoyed seeing the young mums pushing buggies up and down to the shops at the corner. After breakfast she would stand at the living-room window, keeping back a little so as not to appear to be nosy, and would watch the little ones on the way to school. Again, every day at half-past three she would look out for them on their way home, the children dragging their bags and their feet behind them.

Children always brought a smile to Saha's face. She loved children. Children had always surrounded her at home in India: nephews, nieces, neighbours. She loved to sit them on her knee and tell them stories. Sadly, Ragi and Ada had not been blessed with a family as yet.

Here in Britain, of course, there was also the problem of the language. It was not easy to learn a new language at her age. She wasn't sure she even had the heart for it.

Ada had taken her along to a class where she could learn English when she had first arrived. The people there had been very welcoming and kind to her, but Saha had felt vulnerable and awkward. She was not as confident as the younger incomers about trying the strange new words and one day she had ended up in tears.

"Perhaps it is too soon, Grandmother," Ada comforted her. "Perhaps when you feel more at home here."

"Yes." Saha had tried to smile. "Perhaps you are right. Another day."

* * * *

Saha sighed as she dried the last cup from the rack. She looked through the kitchen window. The little bird with the red breast sat on the bird table, watching, waiting.

Saha's heart skipped a beat.

"Oh," she said. "Here you are again, little robin, out on such a wet day, and I have been keeping you waiting. I am sorry."

She opened the fridge door and took a few flaky crumbs of cheese in her hand.

Coming down the back steps carefully, she called to him.

"Come on, pretty one. Come and see what I have for you today."

Saha continued to chat away soothingly in her soft, gentle voice. Slowly the robin drew near, flitting from branch to branch, until at last it made a little hop on to her outstretched hand.

The old lady continued to whisper gently to her pretty little friend. All the greyness, dreariness and sadness of the day fell away. The robin understood her. Language was no problem to him. He returned to her over and over again until he had had his fill of cheese. Then off he went for the morning.

As she turned to go back into the house, Saha was aware of eyes watching her.

There, peering over the bushes between her and the next-door garden, stood a little lad in school uniform.

"Hello," she said with a smile. She was glad that she had learned that word in English.

The little boy looked at her uncertainly and then ran off, without replying, back into his house.

"What a sweet little boy," she said to herself. "He reminds me of my own son, San."

The following day the robin came again for his cheesy breakfast and Saha was once again aware of the same eyes keenly watching from next door as she fed the bird.

This time when she said "Hello" a shy smile came to the little boy's lips. He was intrigued by her little robin friend. Saha could see that.

THE following week was wet and dreary and there was a chill in the air. Winter had arrived in full force. Many birds had left for warmer places, but the little robin would remain.

Although Saha was glad that her little friend with the bright splash of colour on his breast would be staying, she was also concerned that he wouldn't go hungry.

As often as the robin came searching for food, it seemed that the little boy from next door was there, too. He didn't turn away now when he saw her. He smiled, and his smile brightened her day.

One morning, as she opened the kitchen door, she saw that the little boy was standing in his garden already with his mum. In his hand he held some flaky crumbs of cheese.

Saha beckoned to him. His mum nodded and he disappeared, then came through the garden gate and walked up the path.

"Come." Saha nodded, stretching out her hand to him.

She gently took his hand in hers. Then she stood behind him and together they held out his offering to the robin.

"Come on, little robin. Here is my new friend come to feed you today."

Slowly and cautiously, the robin flitted nearer and nearer. He hesitated on a branch above them. Saha continued to speak gently and reassuringly.

Then it happened! Robin landed on the boy's outstretched hand. He hurriedly pecked a little cheese before flying off into the safety of a nearby tree once more.

The boy turned to Saha, his eyes aglow with the wonder of it.

"He came to me!" he exclaimed.

"Yes." Saha nodded. "He did."

And then, quite unexpectedly, he gave Saha a hug and skipped back off to share his adventure with his mum.

Saha wiped a tear from her eye.

"Thank you, little robin," she said.

All would be well now. She had made another friend.

That morning, as she watched the young mums walk their little ones to school, one little boy, whose name she would soon discover was Robbie, turned and waved at her, a big smile on his face. All the way up the street he kept looking back and waving, until he turned the corner and was out of sight.

Saha turned with a smile. Perhaps it was time to try again. After all, if she was going to tell her new little friend all the stories of her homeland, she would need to learn his language. And Robbie would help her, she felt sure of that.

Now, where was that leaflet about the English language lessons? ■

Signs In The Sky

IF you know how to read the clouds and other clues in the air, you'll have a very good idea of the local weather over the next few hours.

Clouds, in particular, have very distinctive shapes and colours which are associated with different weather types.

"If woolly fleeces strew the heavenly way,
Be sure no rain disturbs the sky."

These small patches of fluff, like a flock of sheep scattered over the sky, are cumulus clouds and a sign of settled weather. However, if the "woolly fleeces" look tall or large and are bundled together, they're holding a lot of moisture and may mean rain. When they're small, in a sunny sky, it's fun to spot the different shapes or pictures made by these little clouds.

Not so welcome, at least out at sea, are the mackerel sky and mares' tails, which "make tall ships carry low sails."

Looking like the light and dark pattern of a mackerel's scales, alto cumulus clouds appear when there is a lot of moisture in the air. In winter they can be an indicator of snow. The mares' tails are cirrus clouds, high up and whipped by the wind, foretelling rough conditions ahead.

The grey blanket that covers the sky – and sometimes the ground – on dull days is a stratus cloud. It's flat, low and full of water, bringing rain, drizzle, fog or mist. ●

Illustration by Martin Baines.

An Abstract View

by Rebecca Holmes.

T all started the day we visited the art gallery. Rain had driven us off the beach, and I had this notion that a little culture might be good for the children. The children were fine. Nick, my husband, on the other hand, was less than impressed.

"Do they really call this art?" he muttered.

I glanced anxiously towards a nearby attendant to check she hadn't heard. I liked several of the paintings, though I couldn't have said why. The gallery's atmosphere appealed to me, too, with its ordered calm and white, unfussy walls.

"I suppose it's a modern kind of art," I replied, pondering over an abstract that seemed mainly to consist of an orange splodge set among blue and grey swirls. "It is . . . arresting."

"Should be arrested, more like," Nick joked. "What's it supposed to be, anyway?"

"Maybe it represents heat, in the middle of a cold world," I ventured. "Still, the children seem to be getting a lot out of it. Henry's been staring at that picture over there for the last couple of minutes. What do you think of it, Henry?"

Henry looked at us, then back at the painting.

"All the arms and legs are in the wrong place," he replied with the forthrightness of a nine-year-old. "Can we go to the amusement arcade now?"

Five-year-old Olivia appeared spellbound by a huge canvas of geometric shapes in umpteen shades of red, currently her favourite colour. Since starting primary school a few months ago, she'd brought home a sheaf of masterpieces she'd painted.

Maybe our little girl had an artistic leaning. It would be nice to have an artist in the family. The only things the rest of us ever painted were walls and fences.

Nick nodded towards another picture.

"The perspective's all wrong on this one. Honestly, Kat, you or the kids could do better."

I was wondering how to take that remark when the sun burst through the windows, filling the room with light.

"Quick. To the beach!" Nick said. "I've been itching to build a decent sandcastle ever since we arrived."

Back home, autumn set in with a vengeance. It had its good days, of course, of woodland walks, and kicking through piles of leaves, but mostly it was a case of having my nose to the administrative grindstone.

On the plus side, the office where I worked was near the town's art gallery and museum, which meant I could sometimes call in for a few minutes during my lunch hour.

It was an excellent way to unwind, as my gaze settled on whichever painting caught my eye. Regular exhibitions by local artists ensured there was always something new. I could be transported to different worlds and experiences without having to travel anywhere.

At first I stuck to traditional landscapes of lush countryside or crumbling romantic ruins. Then I tried to appreciate more abstract paintings, despite finding them difficult to understand.

As with the seaside gallery, there were always some I loved, without quite knowing why.

I was contemplating one of these when I became aware of a woman in a long, floaty dress standing nearby. Her auburn hair was pinned up in a bun from which several strands had already escaped.

"What do you think of it?" she asked.

It was only after I'd told her that she introduced herself as the artist of the work in question.

"Goodness, I hope I didn't offend you." I felt the colour surge to my cheeks. "You must think I'm very ignorant."

"Not at all. I'm Geraldine. So long as you get something from a piece of art, that's what matters."

"I must admit, I always feel better in myself and more able to concentrate after I've been here," I told her, as we chatted briefly and told each other a little about ourselves. "It must be wonderful to be able to create something like this."

"Maybe you could take up painting. There are plenty of classes around."

"Oh, no." I shook my head. "I've never been good at art."

Geraldine tutted.

"You don't have to pass any exams, or do it for a living. Just enjoy it!"

I took her business card, but mainly out of politeness. Me? Painting? The very idea.

Olivia, on the other hand, could paint till the cows came home. I'd stocked up on paints and sketch pads from a cheap shop in town, where I also picked up some of a new range of colouring books aimed at adults, which seemed to be in fashion at the moment.

Apparently these were supposed to be relaxing, though I'd only added them to my basket on a whim because they were on special offer.

To my surprise, as I spread out the materials on the kitchen table that weekend, they attracted Nick and Henry, who'd just come in, damp and muddy, from a morning's football practice.

"I can't remember when I last did anything like this," Nick said, once they'd settled down with mugs of tea.

With everyone else there, it seemed only natural for me to follow suit. Soon we were all companionably occupied and I was telling Nick about my conversation with Geraldine, and her suggestion of art lessons.

"I don't see why not," he said. "It might do you good, since all the extra form-filling in your job has been getting you down recently."

"But do I have time? There's always a lot to do at home."

"We'll all help out a bit more. You might feel less tired, too, with an outside interest. Don't think I haven't noticed," he added. "You could set up in the shed. It's got its own power supply, so you can have a little electric heater in there. Give it a try."

I thought it over. It would be nice to do something different, and Geraldine had been so understanding and encouraging. And if I had my own little space into the bargain . . .

"Do you know what?" I said. "I think I will."

THE shed soon became my little refuge, where I could lose myself in a world of my own for a few hours a week. I had to laugh when the family presented me with an outrageously gaudy smock among the usual selection of chocolates, books and scented candles come Christmas. The other members of the class laughed, too, when I wore it to the village hall where the fortnightly sessions were held.

I was glad I'd joined. The class provided friendship in addition to the pleasure of applying paint to canvas, even though I knew I'd never be a "real" artist.

Not that I got to spend much time on my new hobby. Winter brought the usual rash of coughs and colds. After making a good start on doing more around the house, Nick's efforts fell by the wayside when a promotion meant longer hours at work.

There was no doubt the extra money came in handy, but he seemed so worn out when he came home in the evenings.

In contrast, I felt more energised. Nick had been right when he'd suggested an outside interest would do me good.

With half term coming up and the family's finances in a reasonably healthy state for once, it was time to take action.

"We all need a holiday," I told Nick firmly. "You're going to make yourself ill otherwise, and that won't do any good at all."

As he sighed – something he never used to do – I noticed the bags under his eyes, and the way his whole body seemed to slump.

"You're right, love," he agreed. "I was toying with the idea of us all jetting off for some winter sun, but I can only take two or three days off at the moment. That's not enough for travelling far, even tagging them on to a weekend."

"Never mind," I told him, pushing away tempting images of warm, sun-kissed shores. "We can still go somewhere in this country. How about that cottage we stayed in last August, if it's available?"

Luckily, it was, almost as if the place knew it would be needed.

Maybe the weather knew it would be needed, too. Despite being cold, most days were fine, lending themselves to bracing walks on the beach, provided everyone was well wrapped up and didn't mind being sandblasted by the wind every so often!

"This should blow away our cobwebs!" Nick had to shout to make himself heard.

My Folding Bike

I DREAMED of the freedom of cycling along –
Of a carefree and glorious ride,
With the wind in my hair . . . but alas, that was not
How it turned out the last time I tried!
I haven't the balance or swiftness, you see,
Nor the rock-steady co-ordination.
Thus, me and a bike and a road, it would seem,
Are a rather unsafe combination.
So I bought, second-hand, one of those little bikes
That are great for a trip around town.
With tall handlebars and small wheels, they look like
A contraption that might suit a clown!
A twist of the pedals, a turn of a screw,
And a fold of the tall handlebar
All magically render it tiny enough
To pop straight in the boot of my car.
I drove to a nice countryside cycle path –
Very soon I was wobbling along.
My confidence grew; I was happy and free!
(I might even have burst into song).
Oh, people on mountain bikes pointed and laughed;
As for me? Oh, no, I didn't care.
My dream has come true, thanks to my funny bike –
Carefree rides, and the wind in my hair.

— *Emma Canning.*

"What cobwebs?" Olivia shouted back, looking puzzled.

We adjourned to a favourite café for shelter and hot chocolate, where Nick struggled to explain what he'd meant to our daughter, who looked perturbed at the idea that there might be cobwebs lurking in her brain.

"It's just a saying," I reassured her. "There aren't any cobwebs there."

"Then why say there are, if there aren't?" she persisted.

"Because it's a more interesting way of describing what it feels like when your brain needs fresh air."

It was the same with abstract art, I realised when we visited the gallery later. That didn't show what was literally there, but it gave its own interpretation.

Several new paintings were on display this time. I still couldn't have explained most of them, yet somehow I got a deeper sense of satisfaction now. I even recognised the names of a couple of the artists, whom I would never have heard of without the art classes.

After a while, I noticed Henry was fidgeting, while Olivia started to hum to herself. They'd behaved impeccably so far, but clearly it was time to go. Or it would have been, if there had been any sign of their dad.

We found Nick in a room dominated by sculptures, examining a curious-looking object set on a plinth in the centre.

Even when I tilted my head to one side, I couldn't for the life of me guess what it was, nor why anyone would choose to display it in such a prominent position.

When Nick saw us, his words stopped me in my tracks.

"Isn't this an amazing piece of work? Just look at the way the driftwood's been shaped and partnered with the metal, making the best use of both materials."

It sounded double Dutch to me, but then I'd never really warmed to sculptures. What I did notice was that my husband's eyes were lit up in a way I hadn't seen for months.

That, combined with the colour in his cheeks from the recent fresh air, made him look like his old self again.

"What is it supposed to be?" Henry asked his dad.

"I'm not sure. I just know that I like it. I'd love to be able to take old bits and bobs and fashion them into something like this."

I remembered some of his comments from our previous visit. Now the shoe was on the other foot.

There was no doubt in my mind that he could easily make something just as good as this.

Which gave me an idea . . .

∗　∗　∗　∗

"Why not give it a try?" I said, after I told him my idea. "There are bound to be some classes somewhere. It'll do you good to have an outside interest, even if it's just half an hour here and there."

Now it was Nick who looked thoughtful, as we stepped outside.

"I think I will," he said, still having to raise his voice slightly to be heard over the roar of the sea. "Who knows? One day we might even open our own gallery between us, or have our work displayed at exhibitions."

I wasn't so sure about that, but it didn't matter. I knew that it was what we got out of it in other ways that counted.

But first things first.

This sea air didn't just blow away the cobwebs, it also did wonders for everyone's appetites! There was still plenty to get from this holiday, too, such as some delicious fish and chips. ▪

Chartwell, Kent

THE home of Winston Churchill, Chartwell in Kent was purchased in 1922 and the former prime minister lived there for over 40 years. It's now looked after by the National Trust, and you can tour the house and discover the wartime leader's hobbies and love of wildlife. Drop into the studio in the orchard, which is beside the kitchen garden, and discover where Churchill indulged his hobby of painting. You will also see the largest collection of Churchill's paintings anywhere hanging on the walls.

Some of the walls of the kitchen garden were built by Churchill himself and the garden famously produced fruit and vegetables for all of his homes, including 10 Downing Street. The garden was recreated in 2004 and now provides the delightful café at Chartwell with fresh fruit and vegetables.

Wildlife was a big part of Churchill's life and his home at Chartwell reflected this passion. Take time to view the summer house, which he converted into a butterfly house. You'll also notice that the plants surrounding the summer house have been specially chosen to attract more butterflies to the area. ■

143

In Pride Of Place

by Rosie Edser.

C AREFUL, now, love!" Mum called out to me as she rubbed her sleeve over the table top. "That's valuable, you know."

My heart thudded against my ribs. How many times had I heard her say that to me? Now, the dining table I had known all my life was parked in her garage, waiting to be sold off with the other relics of her life at this house. The rest was disposable, easily forgotten furniture, but it was the table that haunted me.

It appeared to resent the way we were dealing with it, like an old retainer about to be retired out of service. It seemed a little insulting to put it with the other items that were waiting to be sold to random passers-by. But the local antiques shop said it was too big and far too damaged to be of any interest to them. We had called a few other possible buyers, but they had offered us silly money.

Mum finalised the decision with a whisper.

"Let it go with the rest of the furniture. Perhaps it will end up with one of the neighbours."

The dining table was far too big for our bungalow. We knew we could squeeze in Mum and all the items she needed – the reclining chair, the bookcase, her million and one photographs – but the table was not essential.

"Do you want to wait inside until things get going?" I called back now. "It's a little chilly out here."

"I'm OK, love," she replied, watching as cars parked in the lay-by, drawn by the prospect of a garden sale.

My mind whirled with memories – doing my homework at the table, struggling with maths problems; watching Mum polish it with beeswax till it shone; Mum and Dad playing cards with my aunt and uncle every Saturday evening. It was a proper bit of furniture. It had been crafted by a firm who had been in business for over a hundred years.

Its legs were sturdy and the surface strong enough to take the weight of a person. We found this out after Dad slipped a disc and had to use it for a bed till he recovered.

The brass wheels would coast it over the carpet to the right place for Sunday

144

Illustration by Andy Walker.

tea, and an extending flap at each side ensured there was enough space for everyone – even the blackest of family sheep.

✶ ✶ ✶ ✶

A guy with an allergy to razors stood close by me. His breath misted in the cool morning air.

"How much for that over there?" He nodded towards the stepladder and my shoulders relaxed.

"A couple of quid?" I replied, unsure.

Obviously I'd sold it too cheap as he didn't haggle with me. He handed over a two-pound coin and took the ladder, leaving me to half sit, half stand against the dining table in a protective stance.

Mum's voice thundered across the decades.

"Girls who sit on tables don't get married."

I had tutted and dismissed her words at the time. Then, when I brought Phil home to meet her for the first time, she'd laid out the best china. He'd then gone the way of men and found someone else at the disco. The table had supported my arms as I laid my head down and sobbed.

Mum slid a cup of coffee across to me.

"I've put a nip of brandy in it," she confided in a whisper. "Don't tell your father."

Yes, if that table could share all the secrets it had overheard over the years we would be able to make a movie out of them. It had taken flower-arranging lessons with us, been there for typing practice on borrowed machines that clunked noisily as we hit the keys. It had seen Christmas present-wrapping every year, and even bore the scars from ends of Sellotape. The table had allowed wallpaper pasting, listened to bad news and to good. It had put up with it all with never a groan or a creak. Just like Mum, when you thought about it.

The man with the allergy to shaving brought his mate over now. This one looked more streetwise. He put his grubby hand on the table and haggled with me down to 150 pounds. As we bartered, my stomach churned with the enormity of what I was doing. I told him that I'd think about it. Then I realised I couldn't imagine telling Mum that it was gone, as if I'd lost a much-loved pet. Her look of disappointment would be too much for me.

The truth was, I couldn't stand to see Mum give up the one item of furniture that she and Dad bought the day they got engaged. It would be like selling the family silver.

Mum brought out the coffee. She reached down for a piece of rag to put under the tray and I handed her the sign that said *All Reasonable Offers Considered*.

"We're not selling the table, Mum. It's too valuable to do that. It's a part of you, and we are going to keep you and the table together."

Mum shook her head.

"But how will you find room for it?"

"The bed in the single room can go to the dump. It sags in the middle and nobody ever stays over at our house, anyway," I said firmly.

"So what will that room be with a dining-room table in it?" she asked.

"Just a cosy room for visitors. What about that? Or Mum's parlour? There may only be space to have one of the leaves out, but I'm sure you'll be quite at home there."

Mum smiled.

"I will be. Very settled. Thank you so much, my darling."

MUM turned back to the garage and berated the last few customers for missing out on the bargains. After an hour or so, there was only a single car load for the dump and one happy dining table.

I put my hand on my mum's arm.

"Tell me something, Mum," I began. "Why did you always say I would never get married if I sat on the table?"

It was something that had always bothered me.

"Oh, I think it was one of your gran's old Irish sayings." She shrugged. "You know. It's the same as, if you don't eat your carrots you won't be able to see in the dark."

"But I did get married. And we're very happy," I pointed out.

"The table must have pretended not to notice, then. And you still can't see in the dark, can you, despite all those carrots I made you eat?" She looked at me

The Shadow

THERE'S a shadow in the garden
Where the tall hedge grows;
A shadow like no other
That quickly comes and goes.
It leaves no track behind it,
Nor makes the slightest sound
As it hurries and it scurries
Across the dew-kissed ground.
Exquisite is the wood mouse
Who comes at close of day,
Watchful of those predators
Who frighten him away.
Tiny, dainty footprints
Moving with such stealth,
Each a perfect work of art,
A pattern of himself.

– Dawn Lawrence.

carefully. "You know, it could go in your dining-room. You could keep the single room as it is. It'll soon be time for your grandchildren to start coming over for sleepovers now they're a bit older."

"Mum, I couldn't."

'Don't be silly. Of course you could," she replied. "Your dining-room would like an antique. Besides, I'm not sure you'd get it through the bedroom door. At least downstairs there are French windows."

We stood, digesting this new change for a moment, then I hugged her.

"So you would still sit in your usual place?"

"If you like."

"Yes, Mum, I would like that very much."

And somehow, there in the garage, I took stock of everything in my own home. The modern furniture, even the odd bits and pieces that had cost quite a lot, could not compare to this piece of mahogany. This was the one item that stored memories safe in its grain. It was much more than its separate parts of wood and hinges. Over the years it had taken on a life of its own and it was as much a part of my parents' marriage as their wedding rings.

One day, I realised, my children would go through all this with me. And if I was very lucky, they would understand how hard it is to cut a home down to what is important in the final years – to those few people, the souvenirs and keepsakes that make us happy.

No doubt they would have to find a new home for the table once again. It would surely grab their hearts as it had mine. And that's what made it a priceless thing of value that I could not sell, whatever the price on offer. ∎

A Foggy Day

OCTOBER can be a surprisingly mild month. Farmers of old used to rely on the "little summer" that was said to occur around St Luke's Day – October 18 – to finish off a late harvest. Soon after, the feast day of St Simon and St Jude, on October 28, would often mark another break in the weather and the onset of gales.

If farmers wanted to know if winter would be harsh, they only had a couple of days to wait to watch what happened to the ducks on their ponds at the end of the month.

"If ducks do slide at Hallowtide,
At Christmas they will swim.
If ducks do swim at Hallowtide,
At Christmas they will slide."

A mild Christmas would follow if the ducks spent their Hallowe'en skating, but a mild start to November meant a freezing Christmas – in theory at least!

November, as the poet Thomas Hood noted, can be a bit gloomy:

"No sun – no moon!
No morn – no noon –
No dawn – no dusk – no proper
time of day . . ."

Fog is particularly common in November, but if you're lucky, this might also be the time that you see a fogbow. A fogbow is a rainbow-like arch, less bright in colour, that forms in fog rather than rain. Like rainbows, fogbows form where there is sunlight and moisture but the sun needs to be low in the sky, so they are most likely to be spotted in the morning or evening. ●

Illustration by Kirk Houston/Thinkstockphotos.

Something To Write Home About

by Annie Harris.

H I, Mum and Dad,
Hope everything is OK. Sorry the weather is so bad. My friend
Josie at uni – she's the one studying medicine – says they've had
a month of non-stop rain. In Provence it's a lovely autumn day:
warm, blue sky, only the leaves on the trees in the peach orchard
next door turning brown to tell me we're into October.

I'm really happy here. Monsieur and Madame (they've told me to call them
Bruno and Orlane, but I don't like to) are lovely. No au pair could ever wish for
nicer employers.

As for the children, they are just gorgeous (most of the time!)

Emilie and Maxime (six and four) are at school. I collect them at 3.30 p.m.

149

and give them something to eat before Maman and Papa get home. By the way, they really loved those chocolate bears and the gingerbread men I brought for them.

They're supposed to speak English with me, but it's usually a sort of "Frenglish".

Alain, Madame's younger brother, is studying English at Marseille University and they also speak English with him. The aim is to make them bilingual, but it's an uphill struggle so far, although it's sweet when Max joins in "Old MacDonald"!

Alain visited last weekend. They were surprised to see him, because he hasn't been for ages, so I suspect it was partly to give me the once-over. I hope he approved!

He looks like Orlane – dark hair, brown eyes, and quite dishy in a French kind of way!

Lily is two and adorable, though a real live-wire, so I'm getting this done while she's asleep in her cot.

I spoke too soon! I can hear her calling.

Give Buster a pat from me. Hugs and kisses to everyone.

Love, Hayley.

＊　＊　＊　＊

Hi, Mum and Dad,

Well, where to begin? I suppose with the neighbour, old Monsieur Piquard (he's a darling), who was sweeping up leaves and burning them when I came past with Emilie and Maxime on Monday. The smoke reminded me of Bonfire Night, so I told them how, in our village, people will be helping to build the bonfire on the green, and the top class in the primary school will be making the guy.

They thought it was hilarious when I told them about that year when you, Mum, sneaked Dad's old suit for them to use and he spotted it on the top of the bonfire!

I said that Mr Walters will soon be busy making his special November 5 sausages for the hot dogs and the WI ladies will be preparing their own-recipe parkin and the cinder toffee for the toffee apples. I remembered how one year that toffee yanked out the loose tooth that I hadn't let Dad pull out for ages – they thought that was very funny, too.

And, of course, I said about Mr Beasley from the New Inn always being in charge of the fireworks.

I had problems with some of the Frenglish. They knew all about fireworks, but toffee apples mystified them at first.

Luckily, Alain was here so he helped translate for me. Anyway, they were very intrigued and told their parents about it over supper.

Which reminds me, I was telling Madame about your world-famous bread and butter pudding, Mum, and she wants me to make it for them some time, so can I have the recipe, please?

I'm a bit nervous, though. Maybe you should make one and send it incognito. Only joking!

Then, a couple of days later, I was just taking E and M into school when the mother of one of their little friends stopped me and wanted to hear all about *la Bonfire Night Anglaise*.

Apparently, her daughter has talked about nothing else since Emilie told her, so I explained about it as we walked home together, pushing Lily in the buggy.

Oh, no, she's just woken up. I shouldn't have mentioned her!

Love and hugs to everybody.

Hayley.

*   *   *   *

Hi, Mum and Dad,

Thanks for the e-mail and the recipe. Haven't made the pud yet, but will have to soon.

Me and my big mouth! I just haven't had the time. When I was telling the children about Bonfire Night I thought that maybe I could organise some toffee apples and a few sparklers (if you can get them here) in the back garden for them, but things have just gone crazy.

I suppose I should have known. As June, a very nice lady who's married to a Frenchman and has lived here for yonks, told me, the French are always up for a party – and they haven't had a fireworks display in the village since Bastille Day, which was months ago!

Anyway, all the children at school have been telling their parents how they want a Bonfire Night, and they've called a meeting at the school to discuss it. It's tomorrow evening and they want me to tell them all about it because they're so interested.

I won't sleep a wink tonight; I'm so nervous. I'm sure every word of French I've ever known will disappear into thin air the moment I get up to speak. What was that I said about me and my big mouth?

Love to everyone,

Hayley.

*   *   *   *

Hi, Mum and Dad,

Thanks for the good luck wishes. I didn't have time to reply yesterday.

Well, it all went brilliantly. I was very nervous. The headmistress was sitting in the front row, but it helped a lot that Alain had come, ready to help out if I got in a muddle.

I managed OK. I told them how it all started, with Guy Fawkes, of course, trying to blow up Parliament on November 5, 1605 (I had to look that up on Google!), then how it's commemorated and about what we do in our village.

They wanted to know everything, and the long and the short is they've decided to have a Bonfire Night of their own on the fifth. They didn't finalise all the details, but I've been here long enough now to know that there will be no half-measures.

The French do love organising things precisely!

Although it went well, I was shattered by the end, so Alain took me off to the village bar for a restoring drink. He says he's definitely going to be here on the fifth, and that he wouldn't miss it for anything. As he said, if he's studying English it's only right that he should get to know our customs, however weird!

Love and kisses,
Hayley.

✳ ✳ ✳ ✳

Hi, Mum and Dad,

It's all over! When I took E and M to school this morning, I could still smell bonfire smoke everywhere. Lots of parents came up to me to tell me how much their family had enjoyed it.

It was such fun last night. It started with some of the children processing to the playing field with candle lanterns, then the little village band (mainly drums and pipes) got things going. The bonfire was huge! Apparently a parent who's a builder had loads of old wood to get rid of. And the guy was enormous and very smart.

Alain whispered to me that it was supposed to be the mayor, but fortunately he didn't seem to recognise himself.

The toffee apples and hot-dog stalls did a roaring trade, helped by gallons of cheap plonk to wash it all down (pop for the kids). The fireworks were really good (not too loud, because of the little ones), and guess who was asked to light the bonfire! Yes, me!

People are already talking about making it an annual event, and Monsieur Henri, the mayor, was floating the idea of our two villages twinning. It's usually only towns and cities that do it, of course, but he thinks it might be arranged, which would be great. I'll be really sad to lose touch with everyone here.

Bruno and Orlane are delighted that it all went so well, and as a thank-you for my efforts they've insisted on treating me to dinner on Saturday at the swishest restaurant round here. Alain is taking me and we'll both have to wear our very poshest outfits.

Talking of Alain, I think I told you that he's coming to England next year to

Bonfire Night

THE quiet lane is thronged for once
With people wrapped against the cold,
All heading down towards the field –
Excitement rife in young and old!
The night sky glows a wondrous red
And soon we feel the fiery heat
And join the people clustered round,
All rubbing hands and stamping feet!
The bonfire blazes, crackles, roars –
We watch with starry-eyed delight
And children wave their sparklers high
As flames and laughter fill the night.
            – Eileen Hay.

do a Masters degree. He has settled on Bristol, which is miles away from my uni, but we can meet up occasionally, despite the distance.

The way the time is flying it will be next summer before I know it and I'll be back home with you, getting ready to go back to uni, catching up with what Josie and all my other mates have been up to. We keep in touch with e-mails, but it's not the same.

Hugs and kisses, Hayley.

P.S. Tell poor old Buster to keep away from that boxer in Lime Crescent. He is bad news.

* * * *

Hi, Josie,

I'm back! How are things in medical school? As you'll have gathered from my e-mails, I had a really great time in France. I was so lucky with my family – they were lovely. I even stayed on through the summer hols to help out with the children. They took us to Sanary, a super little place on the coast.

But now I'm feeling really down. Poor Mum and Dad were so looking forward to me coming home, getting all my favourite food in, doing up my bedroom as a surprise, but ever since I got here I've been a real misery guts, moping around.

Do you medics have anything for a broken heart? It's Alain. I just didn't realise till now that I'd fallen for him in a big way. He's coming to England to do that course, but it's at the other end of the country so I'm hardly likely to bump into him.

I should have read the signs. He was supposed to come to Sanary, then changed his mind, and on the day I left he didn't even come to say goodbye, sending just a one-line e-mail wishing me *bon voyage*.

It's obvious he isn't interested. I think he must have seen me as the equivalent of a holiday fling. He probably had a girlfriend hidden away in Marseille all the time.

Ah, well, plenty more fish, as they say.

Oh, no, an e-mail's just popped into my inbox and it's from Alain. Wiping the slate clean for both of us before our terms start, no doubt. I won't bother reading it. Maybe I'll just have a quick look, though – see what he has to say for himself.

See you Monday.

Hayley.

*   *   *   *

My dear Hayley,

I hope you like my very first selfie and that you recognise the clock tower behind me. I smile to imagine you running past it, looking at the time. I remember you told me you are always late for your lectures! And I remember everything else you have ever told me.

I am so ashamed if I hurt you, but, please, forgive me. I didn't come to Sanary because I was in England! I was attending an interview, hoping that I could change my course to the same university as you. As I was going to have to wait several weeks before I knew, I was afraid I would not be able to stop myself telling you my plan and then have it all go wrong.

You see, dearest Hayley, I knew before you left that even being only 200 miles away would be 200 miles too many away from you. So here I am, standing in the very spot you know so well, waiting for you. If you really can forgive me.

Please e-mail, *chérie*, and tell me that you will be as happy to see me as I shall be to see you.

Bisous, Alain.

P.S. I would love to meet your parents (and Buster). You have told me so much about them.

It will be November quite soon, so perhaps this year I can experience a real English Bonfire Night! ■

St Peter Port, Guernsey

ST PETER PORT is sometimes called the jewel in Guernsey's crown, with its patchwork of architectural styles tumbling down the hills surrounding the port where ancient Castle Cornet stands guard. It is definitely one of the prettiest harbour towns you'll ever see.

It's difficult not to fall in love with St Peter Port's cobbled streets and quaint colourful buildings. Watch out for the barrière stones as you go. They mark the boundary of the town wall – though it is disputed if this was ever actually built – but, more importantly, are the demarcation line between town and country.

Famous for its floral displays, St Peter Port won two gold awards at the RHS Britain in Bloom competition in 2014. From the Old Quarter to the town's seafront, numerous blooms were planted and in the summer they make the town look truly spectacular. ■

A Walk In The Woods

by Gwen Rollinson.

ONLY four months to go," Louise said with a chirpiness that seemed incongruous with a Monday morning.

"Sorry?" I looked up from my computer, which was taking an age to boot up. "Four months until what?"

"Christmas!" Her response suggested that I was being totally thick.

"Lou, it's August. There's bright sunshine outside and I, for one, would rather be lying on a beach than thinking about Christmas."

It was hard enough, in my opinion, being stuck in an office on such a beautiful day.

"Don't be such a grumpling, Evie," Louise teased. "You know how much I love Christmas."

Actually, I did, and I should have remembered, after several years of working with her, that for Louise, thoughts of the festive season always began in summer.

"Just a minute, I'll see if I can dig out last year's tinsel and we'll start the festivities now," I said.

Louise's eyes lit up, until she registered the note of sarcasm in my voice. We caught each other's glances and grinned.

"Sorry, I couldn't resist," I said.

She nodded.

"But these things do take planning," she defended herself.

I sighed. My friend obviously wasn't ready to drop the subject of Christmas just yet.

"What's to plan, Louise?" I pointed out. "A meal for one, a bottle of wine and several boxes of chocolates in front of the telly. Sorted!"

"Evie, you can't spend Christmas Day on your own like that." Louise's voice was full of dismay.

"No option, really, this year. My parents are planning to spend this Christmas abroad; my sister will be celebrating with her in-laws. You're off skiing in France, and everyone else I know is going to be with their families."

"That's sad." Louise looked at me in a forlorn manner.

"I'll be just fine," I said jovially. "Really, I will."

I was secretly unsure whether I was trying to convince Louise or myself.

Thankfully, an e-mail with a query from the warehouse pinged on to my screen, casting all thoughts of Christmas from my mind. Besides, the Yuletide season was months off still – not even worth thinking about yet.

*   *   *   *

Well into November, Louise continued to give me pitying looks every time she raised the subject of Christmas.

Even the rest of the girls in the office were starting to follow suit.

Illustration by Mandy Dixon/Thinkstockphotos.

If I were honest, I didn't enjoy being cast as a Bessie No Mates, but why did everyone think that spending Christmas on one's own was the worst thing in the world?

For all they knew, I might be happy to sit watching a repeat of "The Wizard Of Oz"!

By the time it reached the middle of December it seemed that Louise had all but reserved me a place at the senior citizens' Christmas Day lunch at the Imperial Hotel.

"We must be able to find somewhere for you to go."

She flicked through the pages of the free local paper during our coffee break.

"Louise, will you stop that? I do not need to have my Christmas arranged for me."

I removed the paper from her desk.

"Go to France, ski down some slopes and don't worry about me. Have a lovely time and enjoy the festivities. I'm a big girl and I can manage my own affairs."

"But that's the point," she wailed. "You haven't managed them! You're going to be alone at Christmas, like that chappie in the story with the ghosts."

"You mean Scrooge from 'A Christmas Carol'?"

I was tickled by my friend's simplistic description of Dickens's classic story.

"I'm nothing like Scrooge, and I most certainly don't have a 'Bah, humbug' view on life," I retorted. "Besides, if you recall, at the eleventh hour Scrooge did end up spending Christmas with his nephew."

Louise huffed.

"Oh, well, if you really don't want my help I'll stop."

"Can I have that in writing?"

I caught her eye and we both laughed.

✳ ✳ ✳ ✳

We finished work early that week, three days before Christmas Eve.

It left more than enough time to get ready for the big day, I joked to myself. The fact was, besides a few presents and cards from family and friends, there was nothing in my flat to suggest that the festive season was upon us.

I hadn't even sorted out a tree. I never usually had to think about it as I always had Christmas at my parents' and they took care of all the festive trimmings.

I didn't possess so much as a bauble.

Part of me wasn't sure it was worth going to all the trouble and expense of decorating. As much as I loved the scent of a real Christmas tree, it would be impossible for me to dispose of it afterwards.

Besides, I had to accept that it would only highlight the fact that I had no-one to enjoy it with. Perhaps I should get Louise to phone up the Imperial Hotel after all!

It was while I was debating whether or not to "do" Christmas that the telephone rang.

"Evie? Hello, pet. It's Auntie May. I'm hoping you can do me a massive favour."

My dear auntie May had moved to Honeysuckle Cottage in Devon earlier in the year. The photograph she had sent me looked just like those you used to see on the lids of chocolate boxes.

Although I hadn't yet visited, I could already picture the oak-beamed ceilings and inglenook fireplace clearly in my mind's eye from Auntie May's descriptions.

It sounded like the kind of place I might aspire to owning whenever I got myself a much better paid job or a rich husband – neither of which seemed likely in the foreseeable future!

"Hi, Auntie May, how can I help?"

"I know you'll probably have loads of parties lined up and that this is a terrible imposition, and the last thing you'll want to do is trek over to Devon," Auntie May gushed. "But I wondered if you would like to spend Christmas here?"

Relief washed over me.

An imposition? I had no idea why she thought I would be doing her a massive favour by spending Christmas down in Devon with my favourite aunt.

Auntie May was my saviour, if she did but know it. My eleventh hour had come, just like Scrooge. I wasn't going to be spending Christmas alone after all!

"Of course. I'd love to."

"That's marvellous, darling. The thing is, I've been invited at the last minute to join friends in Italy and it means flying out on Sunday. The kennels which usually take Jasper are full and there's no time to organise anywhere else!" She paused for breath. "I know Jasper would be happy with you looking after him and it would give me so much peace of mind. You are a darling."

Huh, I thought. So much for spending Christmas with Auntie May. I was now spending it with a retriever!

Still, there was really no contest between staying in my lonely flat or a beautiful cottage.

"You don't need to bring a thing. I'll make sure you're well stocked up for a festive Christmas."

She chuckled.

"You might even find an extra surprise in store!"

I WAS still pondering what "extra surprise" Auntie May might have in store for me when I drew up on the drive of Honeysuckle Cottage. Turning off the engine and picking up my phone from the passenger seat, I noticed a missed call. I always mute my mobile when I'm driving so I don't get distracted.

I assumed it would be from Louise. Every day since we had finished work she had either phoned to say she was thinking of me, or had left me a line of kisses in a text – her abridged version of the former.

I pressed the button for voicemail.

"So sorry not to be there when you arrive, darling!" Auntie May's voice rang out. "Snow has been predicted for the area so I thought I'd better set off to the airport earlier. Jasper and the house key are up at the manor. Speak soon, darling."

The house key was up at the manor?

I grinned. Auntie May certainly had made influential friends in the short time she'd been here.

From the directions she left at the end of the message, the manor didn't seem to be that far away, and after being in the car for a few hours I was ready to stretch my legs.

I wrapped myself up in my coat and scarf, thankful that my boots were designed for walking, and set off along the lane.

Snowflakes were just beginning to fall as I swung the knocker on the oak front door. I wondered if anyone would actually hear.

Thankfully, the door opened and a smiling face framed by sleek, black hair greeted me.

"Hello. You must be Evie."

The man extended a hand and beckoned me inside.

I nodded up at him, unable to produce a sound as I found myself looking into the bluest eyes I had ever seen.

Whatever I had been expecting, it certainly wasn't this. I could almost hear Auntie May's voice in my ear saying, "Surprise!"

"I'm Marcus," he continued as I followed him down corridors lined with oil paintings to a large but cosy kitchen.

Jasper was dozing in front of an Aga.

"You certainly have a lovely place here," I managed to say.

"We like it."

He smiled that heart-stopping smile again before explaining that the manor had belonged to his family for generations and that he now helped his parents to run the estate.

Over a mug of coffee he gave me a potted account of how, along with a team of workers, they opened the gardens to visitors in the summer, hosted weddings and functions and farmed the land organically.

"It's a case of having one's finger in as many pies as possible. A house like this is expensive to run."

"I can imagine," I said.

"Your aunt, bless her, has even helped us out when we've been short staffed."

Marcus was easy to chat to and I could have stayed in that warm room for ever, but I knew I should make a move.

Changing Times

WHEN we were young we walked for hours
Around our high street shops.
Then clothes our size were stylish,
Whether dresses, skirts or tops.

We never had to sit down
For a coffee fix or two,
Or rest our aching feet and legs
(Or make sure there's a loo!)

On Saturdays, we loved to dance
Around our ballroom floor.
We'd quickstep, foxtrot, jive and waltz
With energy for more!

These days, we have a bus pass
So we don't have far to walk.
We reminisce with bus-stop friends,
Who always love to talk.

Sometimes we question why it is
Things had to change so much.
Life seemed much simpler years ago.
We now feel out of touch.

We're grateful, though, for many things
Not seen in yesteryear,
So, whatever life may throw at us,
We thank God we're still here!
– *Joan Zambelli.*

"I can run you back in the Land-Rover if you'd like," Marcus said.

I glanced out of the window at snowflakes which were now falling thick and fast.

"That's very kind of you, but I'll be fine walking," I said, even though I had to admit the prospect of spending a little more time in Marcus's company was appealing.

I stood up.

"OK to go out the trade entrance?"

I pointed to a stable door which led out on to a courtyard.

"Absolutely." Marcus grinned.

"Just one thing . . ." he added as I lifted the latch. "Remember to take Jasper with you."

iStock.

161

He pointed to the retriever who stretched unwillingly from his warm spot and stood up.

"Fancy forgetting you," I said to Jasper as we set off down the path. I was still blushing. "Marcus must think I am a real idiot!"

HONEYSUCKLE COTTAGE was everything I could have dreamed of, with its whitewashed rough stone walls and quaint nooks and crannies. Auntie May had left a basket full of chopped logs on the hearth, as well as a store shed full, so, following her written instructions, I soon had a crackling fire going.

On the settee she had also left a couple of boxes filled with Christmas decorations and baubles. All I needed was a tree to hang them on.

Tomorrow, I decided, I would wander down to the village to see if I could buy one.

In the meantime, I was ready for something to eat and I discovered I was spoiled for choice. In the well-stocked larder Auntie May really had provided everything I could possibly want, including a turkey which seemed on the large side for one person.

* * * *

It was Christmas Eve. I woke up to a breathtaking covering of snow, and I couldn't wait to get out into it once I'd fed myself and Jasper. When it came to snow I was still a big kid!

Jasper, for his part, shot outside as soon as I opened the door and seemed ecstatic to be jumping in, over and through it, even though it nearly reached his tummy in places.

Just as I was about to leave for the village, with visions of dragging a large tree back up through the snow, a Land-Rover rumbled up the drive. My heart skipped a beat as I realised it was Marcus.

"This is for you." He unloaded a large tree. "Your aunt bought this from the estate as a surprise for you, with strict instructions that I was to deliver it to you personally. I forgot to mention it yesterday."

"Another business venture?" I asked, helping him to drag the hulking tree towards the cottage.

"Yep." He paused before adding sheepishly, "I was told I had to set it up for you, too."

Manhandling the tree through the front door and into the lounge turned out to be fun as we had to bend it at all angles, and ended up being showered with pine needles. A fit of the giggles overtook us both, especially when Jasper decided to try to help by tugging at the lower branches, and we had to stop several times to compose ourselves.

We eventually wrestled it into a large pot and held it firm with bricks which Marcus found outside. It looked perfect, even without any baubles. Auntie May really had come up trumps. She knew how much I loved a real Christmas tree.

"I think we deserve a hot chocolate after that," I said.

"Sounds good to me." Marcus picked up a shiny red bauble and hung it on a branch.

While I heated the milk, Marcus kindly vacuumed up the trail of pine needles. Domestically capable, I noted – another quality to add to his already numerous talents. I could easily fall in love with this guy.

Before long we were sitting in front of another crackling fire, dunking biscuits into our hot chocolates with Jasper lying at our feet. It was hard to imagine a more idyllic domestic scene.

"Well, I'd better make a move," Marcus said after we'd drained our mugs. "I want to do a quick tour of the estate before holing up for Christmas. I think we're due more snow."

"Of course," I said, showing him to the door, wondering where the time had gone.

It felt like he'd only been here five minutes.

He smiled, his gaze lingering on me until my cheeks tingled, and it felt like one of those moments when there was something important to say, but neither of us said it.

I watched his Land-Rover rumble away down the drive, leaving me and Jasper alone again.

✳   ✳   ✳   ✳

"What do you mean, you didn't invite him to Christmas dinner?" Louise scolded when she phoned later.

She'd taken the trouble to call me from France.

"I thought you said you could manage your own affairs?"

"Come on, Louise. He'll probably have a houseful of people at the manor," I protested, picturing a long table laden with Christmas fare and a room full of laughter.

"You said his parents are away."

"Yes, but he might have offered to do Christmas dinner for the estate workers."

"But you didn't ask."

I could picture Louise rolling her eyes at me.

"No, and he didn't volunteer any information, either. Besides, I wouldn't have wanted to appear pushy. He might have thought I was angling for an invitation."

"Oh, Evie . . ." Louise sighed. "Well, have a nice Christmas with Jasper anyway."

"I will," I said, wishing her a happy Christmas back.

It might be just me, Jasper and a plasma screen television, but I was determined to enjoy the day.

CHRISTMAS DAY brought even more snow, firm and compacted, so that when I stepped outside, after putting the turkey in the oven and laying a place for one at the table, it made a satisfying crunch beneath the wellies I had borrowed from Auntie May.

Jasper followed me out, and before I knew it we found ourselves on the narrow lane bordering the manor.

I let Jasper off his lead as there was no possibility of traffic and, unfortunately, he decided to take full advantage of his freedom. Disappearing through a hole in the hedge, he made off across the snow-covered lawn towards the manor, flatly refusing to respond no matter how much I called his name.

I hurried along the lane and turned in at a gate further along. There was no sign of the dog as I followed the gravel path towards the house.

"Jasper!" I hollered as I caught sight of him sniffing about near the kitchen door.

At that moment the door opened and Marcus stepped out.

"I'm ever so sorry; he just ran off."

"That's all right," Marcus said. He bent down to stroke Jasper's head. "He probably just wanted to wish me a happy Christmas."

"Oh, yes. Happy Christmas."

"Do you have time for a Christmas coffee?" Marcus asked. "That's short for coffee with a shot of brandy and a dollop of cream."

"It's a lovely offer, but I'm sure you have loads to do," I stammered. He was obviously just being polite.

"Besides doing a fry-up for one?" he asked quizzically.

A fry-up?

"The thing is, I thought you'd be cooking a big Christmas dinner," I ventured.

He laughed.

"Hardly. There's only me here."

"You can't spend Christmas on your own!" I said, before I could stop myself.

I was beginning to sound a lot like Louise!

"No option this year," he responded.

He pulled a sad face.

It was time to take the bull by the horns, I told myself, otherwise I could miss another opportunity and then I would never hear the end of it from Louise.

"Well, the thing is, I have an oversized turkey in the oven. If you're willing to help peel some spuds, you're welcome to come to me for Christmas dinner."

There. I'd said it.

My heart had practically jumped into my throat. It was a wonder he could understand a word I said.

"It's a deal," Marcus said, as simply as that.

*　*　*　*

Marcus and I stood in the kitchen of Auntie May's cottage. We were enjoying a glass of wine whilst I made some bread sauce.

"I would have invited you to join me for Christmas dinner when you were here yesterday," I said. "But . . ."

"I nearly asked if I could come," Marcus told me, twisting the stem of his glass in his hands. "But . . ."

We both dissolved in a fit of laughter – helped a little, I suspect, by the wine as well as the situation.

"I've brought a little something to help with the festivities," Marcus said once we'd recovered. "It's in my jacket."

He disappeared into the hall and returned, concealing something behind his back.

"Happy Christmas, Evie," he said, revealing a sprig of mistletoe which he proceeded to hold above my head.

"Happy Christmas, Marcus," I said, reaching up to him.

Well, it would have been impolite not to.

*　*　*　*

"I'm having a lovely day," I was able to tell Auntie May truthfully, when she phoned later.

For her part, she was definitely enjoying her holiday, judging by the merry laughter in the background.

"I'm so pleased. And did you enjoy your little surprise, my darling?" she asked.

"I most certainly did," I told her. "It was wonderful."

But I wasn't just referring to the Christmas tree, as Auntie May would discover when she returned from her holiday.

Thanks to a little help from Jasper the retriever, Christmas at Honeysuckle Cottage had given me more of a surprise than even dear Auntie May had bargained for.

And after spending more time in Marcus's company, I had a sneaking feeling that this might just be the first of many Christmases we would be spending together. ■

Let It Snow

MANY of the cards falling through letter-boxes during the month of December depict a white Christmas, yet in the British Isles, at least, a white Christmas doesn't occur very often.

Although bookmakers define it as a single snowflake falling at a particular location during the 24 hours of December 25, most of us would want to see at least a covering of snow on the day for a proper white Christmas. There is something magical still about seeing snow fall at Christmas – if we don't get too much!

It's true that every snowflake is unique, but they are all a variation on a six-sided hexagon because of the way the ice crystals that form them join together.

One less common form of winter snowfall is thundersnow. Like a summer thunderstorm, this happens when the atmosphere is unstable but the conditions are cold enough to produce snow instead of rain. The lightning can look brighter as it is reflecting off the snowflakes. The snow also has a muffling effect on the sound, so it can be quieter than a summer thunderstorm.

When the sun does break through in winter, it's a welcome sign, according to the old proverb, which says:

"Sun through the apple trees on Christmas Day means fine crop is on the way."

A fine gift to end the year. ●

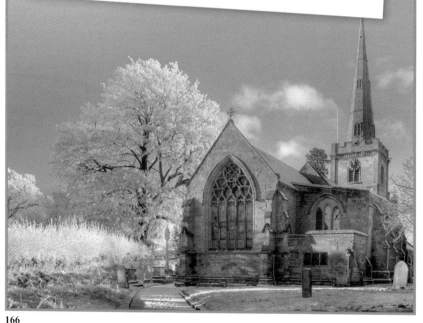

Illustration by Martin Baines.

A Pocket Full Of Snow

by Alyson Hilbourne.

JONAH! It's been snowing!" I called up the stairs.

I heard one thump and then another and then a rumpled four-year-old in Batman pyjamas came hurtling down the stairs towards me.

"Has it, Gran? Really?"

Jonah bounced, his face ruddy, as he rushed over to the living-room window.

Outside, it was still snowing, the lawn already white, and the hedge had a frosting. A thin sun tried to push its way through the clouds.

"Can I go outside?" Jonah's voice bubbled with laughter.

I smiled. My grandson had been quite withdrawn since he'd arrived three days ago.

This was more like his real self.

"Of course."

"Great!" He headed towards the front door.

"Jonah! Breakfast first. The snow will still be there in half an hour, and besides, you're still in your pyjamas."

Jonah followed me reluctantly into the kitchen where his grandfather was already tucking into a boiled egg and toast.

"Snow, eh, Jonah?" Jack said. "Don't get so much of that where you live, do you?"

Jonah could hardly sit still. He wriggled about on his chair, left half his egg uneaten and drummed his feet against the table leg until I released him to get dressed.

"I think we'll leave the washing up," I said to Jack. "We won't get any peace until we get outside."

"Nice to see him more cheerful, though, isn't it?"

Jack nodded in agreement.

We all three of us went out into the winter wonderland.

Jonah scooped up a handful of snow and threw it experimentally at his grandfather.

Jack side-stepped easily, laughing.

I took a photo of them just as Fossil, our ageing black Labrador, bounded over.

"He's trying to catch the snowballs." Jonah giggled, grabbing more snow and throwing it in the air.

Fossil leaped up, snapping at clumps of snow as they descended.

Click, click, click.

I took more photos. Jonah looked so alive and happy.

Then we built a snowman.

"Jonah, what shall we use for eyes?" Jack asked. "We used to use coal when your daddy was a boy, but we don't have a coal fire any more."

"We need a carrot for a nose and some potatoes for eyes!"

Jonah's own eyes shone, and his cheeks were red.

I went to get a carrot and cut a potato in half for the eyes.

"A hat, a hat! He needs a hat!" Jonah shouted.

Jack fetched my straw gardening hat from the shed and brought out an old tin tray that our son had used for sledging when he was Jonah's age. I took some more pictures of Jonah with the snowman.

Jonah shrieked with excitement as he slid down the bank on the tin tray. Fossil leaped about after him, barking.

"I knew it would be worth keeping it." Jack winked at me.

168

How many times had I asked him to clean out the shed?

Nearly three hours after we'd gone outside, we were all wet from the snow, our feet were cold and our clothes soaking.

Jonah was breathless and nearly hoarse from shouting and laughing.

"Come on, get those wet clothes off and sit in front of the fire," I said. "I'm going to make some hot chocolate."

I made toasted teacakes, too, and brought them back with the drinks.

Jonah was staring into the fire and his eyes were moist.

"Jonah, is something wrong?" I asked, looking at him closely.

"Can I stay here, Gran?" he blurted out, wriggling on the carpet. "I don't want to go home. It's all going to be so different, and . . ."

"And?" I prompted gently.

"And this has been the best day ever with you and Grandpa!"

I nodded and swallowed.

What could I say? I couldn't pretend his life wasn't going to be different from now on.

"We've got tomorrow," I said, "and maybe another day before you go home. Let's enjoy them, eh?"

That evening, when Jonah was in bed, I went to answer the phone in the hall. It was our son.

"That's marvellous news!" I said. "I'm so thrilled. A girl! Yes, of course I'll tell him. No, everything's fine. Love to Lindsey. Take care."

Oh, dear. I had to tell Jonah in the morning that he had a baby sister. Somehow I didn't think he was going to be thrilled by the news.

As I went back down the hallway I noticed a puddle of water under Jonah's coat.

Tutting to myself, I carried it into the living-room to dry by the fire. I couldn't have checked carefully enough earlier.

NEXT morning Jonah was up early.

"Can we go out in the snow, Gran?"

"After breakfast. Your daddy phoned last night, Jonah. He wanted me to tell you that you have a new baby sister."

Jonah was silent. His lips trembled.

"What is it, Jonah? It'll be lovely having a little sister to play with."

This time the tears began to trickle down his cheeks.

"Davy Johnson says that all babies do is sleep and cry. His mum was so busy she didn't have time to help him build his Lego castle."

The words were stuck in his throat and he coughed.

I pressed my lips together. Davy Johnson sounded something of a know-it-all, I thought.

"Come here, love," I said, pulling him towards me in a hug.

A Winter Wonderland

A LITTLE winter wonderland –
It's just as I remember:
A vibrant, snowy scene that I
Revisit each December.
I love to see the log cabin
Amidst the frosted peaks.
And children skiing just outside
With smiles and glowing cheeks.
The fir trees, straight and glossy green
Stand proudly in the snow;
A tiny robin redbreast pecks
The icy ground below.
A snowman wears a jaunty hat
With holly round the edge,
Nearby, there's Father Christmas
And a penguin on a sledge!
I'm gazing proudly at the scene
I've lovingly created.
It's finished! Yes, my Christmas cake
Is iced and decorated!

– Emma Canning.

"Of course your mummy will have time to play with you! You're right, babies do take a lot of time at first, but they soon grow up and then you'll have a friend to play with."

I tickled him under the chin.

"Your daddy had a baby sister, too, you know. Your auntie was his baby sister. You like Auntie Polly, don't you?"

Jonah looked up at me, wide eyed, and nodded.

But then he gulped.

"But it'll all be different."

Tears rolled down his face.

"I want to stay with you, Gran. I don't want to go home."

"I know, my love."

I hugged him tight and rocked him a little.

I wondered if Jonah's father had felt like this when Polly was born. It hadn't occurred to me before now.

I hesitated.

I didn't want to tell Jonah any lies. The baby would undoubtedly bring about changes.

Fortunately, at that moment Fossil pushed his nose in between us.

"I believe Fossil wants to go out for a walk," I said. "Shall we go and get our coats on?"

I took the camera with us.

Fossil jumped in a ditch and scurried along the bottom, sending up a volcano of loose snow.

Jonah clapped his hands in delight.

"I wish it snowed where I live, Gran," he said.

"It does sometimes."

"No, it never does," he said sadly.

When we got back to the house, Jack was standing on the doorstep.

"Your mum is out of hospital, Jonah, so Dad is coming to get you tomorrow."

I winced as I saw Jonah blink hard.

The snow in the garden was patchy, partly from where we'd been scooping it up yesterday and partly where it was beginning to melt.

The snowman stood on the front lawn with my gardening hat at a rakish angle.

"Are you coming in for lunch, Jonah?" I asked.

He squeezed his lips together, stuffed his hands in his pockets and looked around.

"I'm going to say goodbye to the snowman," he said, digging into the snow with the toes of his boots.

"OK. Come in soon, eh?"

I went inside and took Fossil with me to dry off his paws.

When I looked out again I was surprised to see Jonah stuffing snow in his coat pocket.

"Jonah," I said gently when he came to the door. "Can you leave the snow outside, please?"

He shook his head fiercely.

"No! I want it. For remembering. We don't get snow in London."

I bit back a smile.

I couldn't argue with his logic. I knew they didn't get as much snow as we did.

"Well, the snow won't stay in your pocket, will it? It'll melt. We'll have to find some other way to remember this holiday."

He looked crestfallen, back to the unhappy child who had arrived five days earlier. The snow had broken through his misery, but the gloom looked set to return.

"I know!" I said brightly. "Let's use the photos I took. We can make a book of 'rememberings' instead. You can help me choose some photos to print this afternoon, Jonah."

We chose some pictures. Jonah making a snowman. Fossil catching snowballs. Jack and I apparently standing in a listing garden – Jonah took that one – and Jonah having fun on the tin tray sled.

We cut out some snowflakes from paper to decorate the book. It looked very good and Jonah was pleased with it. He took it to bed and put it under his pillow for the night.

When I went in to check on him later he was fast asleep, with his rememberings.

I didn't sleep well, however. It wasn't only Jonah who'd enjoyed himself these last couple of days. I was going to miss him, too.

He at least was going to go home to a busy house, but ours would seem empty with just Jack and me rattling around in it.

IN the morning I made Jonah's favourite breakfast of pancakes. He was very subdued.

Around eleven o'clock his father arrived. He showed us pictures of the baby.

"Look, Jonah. This is Mummy with her. See how little her fingers are. You were that small once upon a time."

Jonah chewed his lip and was quiet, but his dad hardly noticed, he was so full of the new baby.

"Jonah, take your father out and show him the snowman," I suggested.

"Do you want to see it, Dad?" Jonah asked.

"Of course – let's go!"

I sighed with relief. At last he'd noticed Jonah.

Soon father and son were laughing together and trying to repair the melting sculpture.

I made them lunch, trying to postpone the time when they would have to leave. It was a long drive back to London and I didn't want them driving in the dark, but on the other hand I didn't want them to go, either.

"Mum, we have to go now," my son said eventually. "Come on, Jonah. Is your bag ready?"

We all trooped outside, into the fading light.

I stood on the front step and I could feel the ache in my chest.

Jonah gave me a big hug, and I had to blink back the tears from my eyes. I didn't want to upset him just when he seemed a bit more cheerful.

As he walked off down the path, clutching his book of "rememberings" in one hand and talking with his father, Jack and I waved goodbye.

My arm was heavy and my vision blurry. I brushed a tear from my face just as Jonah turned to wave back.

Then he was running back down the path towards us, a four-year-old whirlwind of limbs and energy.

"Gran! You're crying!" he exclaimed.

I shook my head.

"I'm not," I said, furiously rubbing my cheeks with the back of my hand. "I'll miss you, Jonah. We've both loved having you here."

Jonah nodded seriously.

"You need some rememberings, Gran," he said, holding out his book. "Davy Johnson says his baby rips things up. Will you – can you keep my book safe for me?"

There was a lump in my throat as big as a mountain. Perhaps Davy Johnson knew something, after all.

"I'll keep it safe for you until you come back again," I said. "You'll be back soon, and with your sister, too."

He pouted slightly and turned to walk back to the car.

I hugged the book we had made.

Perhaps I'd put it under my pillow tonight. I knew he'd be back in the spring and we'd be able to add to the rememberings. His father's fishing net was in the shed.

There would be frogspawn and tadpoles in the pond, I was sure. I would just have to make sure he didn't try keeping them in his pocket . . . ■

Whalsay, Shetland Islands

KNOWN in Shetland as "Da Bonnie Isle", Whalsay is a small island, just five miles long and two miles wide. The tidal sounds and off-lying rocks around Whalsay are among the best places in Shetland to see porpoises and occasional dolphins, Minke whales and orcas. It's easy to understand why the Vikings called it "Hvals-oy" – the island of whales.

There has always been a German influence on the island; for hundreds of years the salt fish trade was in the hands of German merchants. Drop into the museum at Symbister Pier House to discover how ships from Hamburg, Bremen and Lübeck sailed to Shetland every summer, bringing seeds, cloth, iron tools and hard currency.

Fishing is still big business in Whalsay and the harbour at Symbister is home to small creel boats and big ocean-going trawlers alike. The inner harbour is packed with colourful dinghies and the distinctive "Shetland Model" boats which compete in local sailing and rowing races. ▧